WANDA AND THE WELLS OF MARS

A Children's Novel by

Pat Davis

Pat Davis

authorHOUSE®

AuthorHouse™
1663 Liberty Drive
Bloomington, IN 47403
www.authorhouse.com
Phone: 1-800-839-8640

© 2009 Pat Davis. All rights reserved.

No part of this book may be reproduced, stored in a retrieval system, or transmitted by any means without the written permission of the author.

First published by AuthorHouse 12/29/2009

ISBN: 978-1-4490-5940-8 (e)
ISBN: 978-1-4490-5953-8 (sc)

Printed in the United States of America
Bloomington, Indiana

This book is printed on acid-free paper.

To my husband, Joseph, without whose help this book would never have been written, and for my granddaughter, Amber, who was my inspiration.

Wanda and the Wells of Mars
By Pat Davis

Table of Contents

Chapter

1. Suits for Space 1
2. Freedom's Flight 8
3. Gravity of the Situation 19
4. Asteroid or Moon? 27
5. Touchdown on Mars 33
6. Station #2 Awaits 40
7. Oven for Dirt 45
8. Repairs First 51
9. Julia Joins 61
10. Trial Run 68
11. Deep Waters 78
12. Ice is Nice 83
13. Face on Mars 89
14. Problems Galore 98
15. Passageway to the North 105
16. Northern Tablelands 112
17. Chinese Greenhouse 119
18. Secret Mission 125
19. Water for Wanda? 132
20. Coming and Going 137
21. Goodbye Mars 144

Chapter One
Suits for Space

THE NASA OFFICIAL pulled Wanda along to a strange elevator.

"It's not like the elevator for sightseers." The door closed behind her. She faced three astronauts in different sizes – like the three bears – a tall one, a middle-sized one and a short one.

I feel like Goldilocks. Wait till they find out I don't belong.

They stood in spacesuits, toothpaste-white like hers. Their helmet shields of black plastic hid their faces.

"Looks like we have our fourth man for the trip to Mars," Glen said as the elevator surged upward. Wanda gripped the silver railing.

It's my brother, Glen's, elevator for the trip to Mars, Wanda realized, *and he's the middle-sized bear.*

THE NASA OFFICIAL PULLED WANDA
ALONG TO A STRANGE ELEVATOR.

'"You're William Runner, right?," Glen said. Wanda tried to shake her head, 'no', as the elevator suddenly stopped. Her head shook 'yes' instead. They crammed into a White Van and sped to the space shuttle. Buckled into a soft chair, Wanda felt herself sinking into the chair's stuffing as the shuttle rose. She held her breath. The space station, orbiting Earth, grew larger as they approached. Wanda smiled to herself.

I may be thirteen, but my brother's spacesuit fits me just fine, Wanda thought. *Glen was nine when he wore this suit to Mars back in 2044. Now I'm going to Mars in it. Mom let me take the NASA tour because she wanted me to bring home Glen's old space suit. I had to promise to take a pill and call her to get me if I got a migraine.*

Starting and stopping made talking impossible. Then everything was calm. The round door of the space shuttle twisted open as Glen pulled its metal handle. Releasing the straps of her chair, she floated through the door with the others.

Hand over hand, they pulled themselves into and through a small space station. Two men nodded and helped them through another round door. The mouth of the spaceship swallowed them.

"Welcome aboard, Will," the short astronaut said as they floated to gray chairs. "This is our 30 by 40 foot, silver ship, named 'Freedom' with all the comforts of home."

"When your mother saw our ship, she wanted you to come with us," the tallest astronaut said. "Then she changed her mind."

"I guess she let you come," Glen said, "when we told her there would be a woman teacher in our party, to give you lessons. We're meeting her on Mars."

Who is this William Runner kid? Wanda wondered. *Why would they want some other kid to go with them to Mars instead of me?*

The men strapped themselves into the soft gray chairs. Glen helped Will fasten his seat belt. Wanda let him.

"Don't worry, Will," Glen said. "In a few minutes we'll be off." Wanda's words did not come out of her mouth. Her whole body was shaking.

"Now we can take off our helmets," The tall astronaut said. He pulled off his helmet to show hair, dark and wavy; eyes, a piercing, deep blue; and skin, rough and red like a meat-counter chicken. "I'm Jim Rudolf."

Glen removed his helmet and introduced himself to William Runner. His light complexion, pale blue eyes and blonde hair matched Wanda's own.

The short astronaut took off his helmet to show skin like chocolate candy and tight black curls. He looked at Wanda with gentle brown eyes.

"I'm Mark James. We hoped your mother would let you come."

Wanda fumbled with her helmet fastening. Glen helped take off the helmet.

"Wanda!" Glen said. Tears brimmed in Wanda's eyes. "What are you doing here?" Turning to the others, Glen explained, "She's my sister."

Wanda's tears became a waterfall. Glen glared at her.

"I thought that suit looked familiar," he said, "with NASA's name printed in blue instead of black. That's the suit I wore on my first trip to Mars. You were supposed to take the suit home for me, Wanda."

"Glen, go easy," Jim said. "We can turn back to the space station. She can wait in the station for the descending aircraft."

"Wanda, stop crying and tell us how you got here."

"I - I was on the NASA tour when you gave me your old suit to take home. I just tried the suit on." She wiped her eyes. "This NASA official pushed me onto your elevator. I tried to tell him I was with the tour."

"Before we do another thing," Mark said, "let me radio home base. They may be looking for her right now." Mark radioed the base at Dallas. He talked quietly for a few minutes.

"Jim, our sponsors don't want us to turn back. They were disappointed that the other kid, William Runner, was not coming. Since you are our captain, it's up to you to decide what to do with Wanda."

"Wanda, shall we take you back or do you want to go with us?" Wanda looked up with red eyes.

"I can go with you?"

"If you want to," Jim almost whispered. "Your brother, was younger than you when he went to Mars – right Glen?" Glen nodded his head.

"Why do the sponsors want me to stay?"

"They want to see how living in space will affect a child."

"Mom and Dad will be angry with me." Wanda tried to keep from sounding too happy. She remembered how her mother made her go to bed every time she had a migraine.

"Wanda, make up your mind." Glen said. "You always said you wanted to go to Mars. We have enough provisions. It's William Runner's hard luck that he didn't make it. If you want to go back home, you have to decide now, or we will go on."

"Glen, Jim - I do want to go to Mars, but mother is right," Wanda moaned. "She says I'll miss a lot of school - and Glen, you know I get migraines." Tears washed Wanda's cheeks again.

Wanda remembered her mother saying; *"What good would you be on Mars, if you have to sleep for a day. You know how sick you get. If you vomit in your space suit, you could die."*

Chapter Two
Freedom's Flight

"MOM TOLD ME my migraines would keep me from going to Mars." Wanda could not stop her tears. *I wanted to go to Mars – but now I'm not sure. Being on a spaceship is scary. Mom is right.*

"We'll have NASA ship your medication," her brother, Glen said. "Don't worry, I'll take care of you." Wanda wiped her tears and frowned. *I can take care of myself,* she thought.

"We arranged for a teacher to join us on Mars," Jim said. "NASA will send the Math and Science programs on your level."

Now they're treating me like a child, Wanda thought. *I don't need a teacher! I know how to study! I'll show them.* She smiled at the men.

"All right, I'll come to Mars with you."

Mark returned to the radio. Jim and Glen each gave a sigh and began the routine of checking the instruments.

I've wanted to do this all my life, Wanda thought. She floated over to the window near Mark's radio. Looking at the bright stars, Wanda thought about the "Good-bye" party her family had for Glen. *I iced his cake and made him a card with the list of things he should do on Mars.*

"Glen," Wanda said, "remember that list I gave you? My friends, Sue and Latonya helped me write things for you to do on Mars. The first thing we wrote was: 'find water – but more than you can squeeze out of permafrost.'"

"Wanda," Glen said, laughing, "that's our main mission – to search for water in craters. NASA has pictures of Martian craters, with clues that water is present. Some cliffs show shifting ground that NASA believes is due to underground water." Jim joined them.

"Wanda," Jim said, "there are low places, that look like the cracked surfaces of dried lakes. NASA thinks most water may be found in Mars' Southern Hemisphere. That's where we're going – to the Southern Hemisphere of Mars."

"Jim," Mark said from the radio, "the NASA base at Dallas, knows Wanda Roland is replacing William Runner, as the child going to Mars." He turned to Glen. "Your parents are sending a computer video for Wanda. We should have the video in an hour."

"How can they send such a thing in space?" Wanda asked.

"NASA sends a radio message to our radio," Mark said. "We convert the message in the ship's main computer. A program changes the information into a digital picture with sound. Then we send the complete picture to a small computer for you, Wanda."

"I'd like to send a picture of me to Sue and Latonya." Wanda smiled and drifted over to the back window to watch the Earth grow smaller. *My friends! They only became my friends when they found out my brother was going to Mars. I don't need anyone. I do things by myself. I could even find water on Mars.*

Wanda heard Jim talking to Mark and Glen.

"We have to give Wanda a private room. How about using the recreation room? We can move the exercise bikes and the vacuum treadmill up into the main part of the ship." The men disappeared into a hole in the floor at the left side of the ship. They brought two silver exercise bikes and a green box from below.

"We'll bolt the bikes into the floor, here, next to the chairs," Jim said. "We'll fasten the green box behind them."

Wanda floated over to watch them.

"In space," Mark told Wanda, "these machines are as light as a newspaper. Bolting the bikes to the floor is not the hardest part. The hardest part is holding ourselves still long enough to do the work."

"You men remind me of fish wiggling every time you turn a wrench." Wanda said, laughing.

"It doesn't help," Glen said, grabbing a runaway wrench, "for the tools to float away – it's dangerous." Wanda looked about the crowded space ship and laughed.

"There's not much space in this spaceship." *I can just see the wrench floating in here,* she thought. *It bumps into the chair leg. It spins around and undoes the screws that fasten the legs to the padded floor. Oh, no! The chair is loose! It's moving toward the window. The chair crashes through the window. The vacuum of space sucks me through the window. Help!* Wanda floated to the window, laughing as she pressed her nose against the thick window-pane. *The stars are bright in the blackness of space. Our ship is a silver necklace hanging in dark space. It seems like we aren't moving! At least in a moving car, on Earth, I see trees and houses moving past me.* Wanda searched the blackness. *I can't see Earth anymore!* She slapped her forehead. *Of course not! I need the window at the ship's back!* She was swimming to the other end of the ship when Jim called her.

"Wanda, muscles can become too weak in zero gravity. We have to exercise every day. Our space ship doesn't have artificial gravity." Wanda looked at her arms and legs.

"Why didn't you want artificial gravity?"

"Ships with artificial gravity have an outer shell that revolves. This makes an extra pull, called the *Coriolis force*. It's the same force on our turning Earth, that causes the drain water in the Northern Hemisphere to run counter-clockwise, and the Southern Hemisphere water to circle in a clockwise pattern."

Glen joined them.

"NASA still has problems with the 'Coriolis force,'" he said. "In a rotating ship, the 'Coriolis force' can cause you to get dizzy, just by turning your head to look behind you."

"I'm glad we don't have artificial gravity," Wanda said. "Getting dizzy brings on a migraine."

"Besides," Mark said, laughing, "those ships are too big for just four people – and expensive."

"We do have some artificial gravity with the vacuum treadmill," Glen said. Wanda looked around.

"But I don't see a treadmill."

"It's inside that green box," Jim said. "You climb in the box, and with the push of a button, you can fasten its plastic rim around your waist. Another button instantly pulls out the air. Your feet touch what seems like solid ground, but is really a small treadmill. Inside that box, a vacuum allows you to feel your weight as we do in gravity."

"But I'll get dizzy in that vacuum treadmill."

"No, no," Glen said. "You would be in it, only from the waist down."

"We also have a three-foot wide bath cylinder," Jim pointed to another hole in the floor, "that goes from one wall to its opposite wall. For a bath in the cylinder, you're sprayed with water from all sides. A vacuum draws out the water when you're finished."

"Our toilet works the same way," Mark said, "when you flush. It's scary at first, but then you don't need paper."

"We recycle our water, but we can't waste it." Jim said. "You should take no more than ten minutes for your bath, or we have to wait before we get water for anything else."

"But why can't I just take a tub bath?" Wanda asked.

"The water wouldn't stay in a tub in zero gravity," Jim said. "It would float in the air of the ship in many small spheres, like this." Jim opened his plastic drinking bag, to let out a little water. The water formed into a ball floating in the air and quivering. He grabbed the ball of water in his mouth.

"At least, I can still swallow," he said.

"Why can't I use a sponge?" Wanda asked.

"A sponge would be alright, if used inside the cylinder," Glen said, picking up a small computer. "You would still have tiny balls of water floating around. The sponge would be harder to control."

Glen took the computer down to Wanda's new four-foot room. Wanda followed him. He connected the computer wire to one of many computer outlets, sewn into the quilted wall of the ship.

"Our central computer can send information to this small computer through wiring in the ship's walls." Glen pulled a black bag from his belt. "Wanda, these disks hold information about Mars, and here are blank ones you can write on." Glen fastened the zippered bag onto the wall by the computer.

"Be sure to keep your disks in this bag. We don't want them floating around. You have three hours before we eat dinner. Now you are ready for our parents' message."

No, I'm not ready, Wanda thought, *but I won't tell Glen.* "Thanks, Glen," Wanda said, kissing him on the cheek. She pushed a Mars disk into the computer. *This disk holds the words of a whole book. I can erase it and reuse it*, she thought.

"The first trip to Mars, by humans," Wanda read on the little computer, "was made by the Roland family, in 2041." *I was born in 2045, the year after they returned to Earth.*

Wanda's thoughts were interrupted by a screeching sound. She stopped reading her computer and floated upstairs.

"Hurry, Wanda," Glen called. He took her arm. Grabbing the handles that dotted the wall, he followed the others. They were swimming down another hole in the floor. Wanda hadn't noticed it before. After they were in, Glen turned a round metal door to seal the tiny room. A wall lamp showed a narrow space with seats on both sides. They strapped themselves onto the seats. Mark handed Wanda and the others, small lap computers.

"The first program will explain what is happening," he said. "Wanda, your programs are also on yours. I downloaded them in case something happened to your computer."

"This is an emergency," Jim said. "Mark got a notice from Earth about a storm on the sun. He just had time to gather the computers before sounding the alarm."

"You have good reflexes, Wanda," Glen said. "I was just about to get you when you came out of your room."

Wanda opened her computer to find the explanation for their emergency.

"Storms on the sun cause deadly particles from the sun to enter the walls of our spaceship. The special room has thick walls to keep out these particles." Wanda looked at the picture that showed the way the particles moved.

"How long do we have to wait here?" she asked.

"Until the 'All-Clear' siren sounds," Jim said. "Relax and read your computer programs." Wanda sighed and brought up her program again.

"Dave and Betty Roland, and their nine-year-old son, Glen, were sent to Mars by Llyons Aircraft and a group of business investors, with NASA's help. They collected soil and rock samples and did science experiments. They also planted gardens and found fossil signs of ancient life on Mars."

Wanda stopped reading when the siren sounded again. Everyone closed their lap computers. Jim led the way out of the little room. Wanda went back to her little room. The signal of her parents' message was on her computer screen. She put a blank disk in the computer to download the message as she watched it.

"Wanda," her mother's voice said, "we are surprised that you are on your way to Mars." *I know they will be angry,* Wanda thought. She gritted her teeth.

The image, on the computer monitor, made Wanda smile. Her mother was pushing brown curls from eyes as navy blue as Wanda's shorts. Wanda was sure she saw tears, ready to spill.

"Was there a mix-up?" her mom asked. "We wondered why you did not get off the bus at 5:00." Her father smiled, that crooked smile that meant he loved her.

"We wish we were going." he said. "I'm happy for you. Be sure to mind your brother. We will be getting Mark's reports on your journey." They gave her advice and told her they loved her.

Wanda smiled. *It was a nice message. My parents weren't angry with me. They didn't even mention my migraines. I'll play their disk whenever I get homesick.* Wanda labeled the disk, "My Parents", and put the disk in the black bag bulging with the disks about Mars.

She sighed and suddenly felt very tired. Deciding to rest, she undid her seat belt and floated over to her sleeping bag. A terrible feeling came over her. *The sleeping bag is only half there!*

A STRING OF COLORED LIGHTS, SHAPED LIKE TRIANGLES, FORMED A SEMI-CIRCLE. THEY ARE EVERYWHERE I LOOK.

Chapter Three
Gravity of the Situation

"PART OF THE sleeping bag has disappeared!" Wanda looked around the room. *The blond girl in the mirror, only has one blue eye.* Wanda always found it surprising. *No 'hole' ever appears where the missing part should be. The surrounding scenery swallows missing parts.* Wanda just got used to things disappearing, when a string of colored lights, shaped like triangles, formed a semi-circle. *They are on the wall, and everywhere I look.* Wanda knew what that meant – *Migraine!*

The dancing lights are only in my mind. They're caused by pressure from veins in my brain. It always happens when I've had a lot of stress. My favorite aunt got migraines – but hers were caused by allergies.

Wanda reached into her pocket for the small bottle of white migraine pills. *I'm glad Mom had me take the whole bottle. She said no one will question my need for the pills. The doctor's orders are right on the outside.* Wanda clamped her hand over the bottle top as tiny pills started to float out. She made herself swallow the round pill and felt it tunnel down inside her chest. *Next time I'll have water handy,* she thought.

Wanda stretched out inside a green bed bag, fastened to the wall like a butterfly's cocoon. Drifting into sleep, Wanda remembered Glen's handicap. *I might have migraine headaches, but Glen's right foot is false. He was only five when he lost his foot in a car accident. He has more trouble than I do, but it doesn't make him an invalid. A migraine should not make me an invalid.*

Wanda opened her eyes. *The 'lights' are gone. The room is all there.* She heard the men talking. *I must have slept for three hours.* Pulling herself out of her room, she rose to the huge room above. The men floated about like dandelion seeds in a gentle breeze. They were nibbling on hot dog buns.

"Wanda, come here," Mark said. He pulled himself to four doors in the side of the ship. "I'll show you how to get your food." He slid open a glass door, removed a package and shoved the package inside another door.

"This is the super conductive oven," Mark said, reopening the built-in oven to hand Wanda her hot dog. "And here's your orange juice." Mark said, taking a small bag from another door, marked "liquids." "If you are still hungry, help yourself to dried fruit and nuts from this fourth door."

"Thanks Mark," Wanda said. "Sorry I was so late coming to dinner. I had a migraine. I didn't mean to sleep so long."

"It's not your fault," Glen said. "I was afraid you'd get one - too much excitement. We'll send for more of your pills in our first shipment from Earth. Speaking of pills, you need to take this one." Glen gave his sister a square blue pill. "It will help keep the calcium in your bones. Our parents were the real guinea pigs. They took them on the first trip to Mars."

"It tastes horrible. Do I have to take these pills?" Wanda asked. "Couldn't I just exercise?"

"No," Glen said. "Exercise helps, but it's not enough. Since people first began traveling in space, scientists found that their bones loose calcium. It's because of the lack of gravity in space. Gravity helps bones keep their calcium, because muscles work harder and pull on bones. The vacuum treadmill gives you a feeling of gravity. On that first trip to Mars, we only had that treadmill coming back home. You need both the pills and exercise."

"Losing bone calcium makes bones break easily," Jim said. "and you also need strong muscles to walk on Mars."

"Here's how you fasten into a bike," Mark said, strapping himself in the stationary bike. Wanda smiled.

I wonder what would happen with a real bike. I can see it sailing around in the ship with me on top, like a bucking bronco.

"Wanda, your brother was telling us what a good cook you are," Mark said. "I'm the official cook. You can help me."

"I'd be happy to. Just tell me what to do." Wanda bit the end off of her hotdog. "This meat doesn't have much taste," She said, sipping orange juice through the narrow end of a clear plastic bag. "This orange juice doesn't taste good either."

"I'm afraid that's one of the problems with space travel. Our taste is partly lost. We'll have it back when we get to Mars – and gravity." Mark took Wanda's hand and led her to six boxes of plants, fastened to the wall. A plastic lighted hood covered them.

"Why are the plants beginning to grow in all directions?"

"They've been in space without gravity for about a month before we got here," Mark said. "Without gravity, they grow in all directions. They do already have tomatoes on them. Wanda, it will be a big help if you take care of our tomato and spinach plants."

Next to the plants stood a clear plastic box with gloved holes.

"That box reminds me of the incubators I saw at Dad's hospital," Wanda said. Mark laughed.

"I chop the plants inside this plastic box and bag them for salad. You just need to turn the lights on and off and check the plants for water every day. The plants have their roots in water."

"What keeps the water from floating out?"

"A plastic film stays on top of the water even when the water level rises and falls. You squirt more water into this tube. Be sure to clip the tube shut again when you finish. But Wanda, you'll only need to refresh the water once a week. This special water has minerals and food the plants need."

"You want me to help cook and take care of plants?" Wanda asked. "I won't have time to exercise." Glen joined them.

"Mark will have time to concentrate on his hospital skills if you take care of the plants and cooking. The food on the ship is prepackaged. You just warm each package like Mark warmed yours. It shouldn't take too long." Jim floated over to them.

"We'll also let you pass out the drinks. We save our personal water bags and refill them with the recycled water. Be sure to write your name on yours."

Wanda decided she wasn't going to let the men think she couldn't do the work.

"When we get to Mars, I can do more kinds of cooking. Mom taught me how to make bread."

"And I'm going to let her," Mark said.

"Great," Jim said, "I'm looking forward to that. My wife liked to bake bread. I had a hard time leaving her and our three boys, and with one on the way. We'll be gone for three years. I know how ancient sailors felt, crossing the ocean in small sailboats. Their journeys sometimes took more than three years."

"At least," Wanda said, "you got to say good-bye to them. I didn't get to say good-bye to mine. Anyway, you'll be able to see your family with the messages on computers."

"Wanda, if you said goodbye to Mom and Dad, you wouldn't be here." Glen was laughing.

Well, maybe I could have talked them into it, Wanda thought, sticking her tongue out at her brother.

"I told my parents, 'goodbye,' but that was hard," Mark said, "and, well, there was this girl. I met her when we were both studying to be astronauts. She was in a lower class. I'm going to look her up when we get back."

"Wanda," Glen said. "Mark James is twenty years old. He graduated from college, one of the youngest in his class." Mark took a bow that turned into a summer-salt as he floated.

"Wanda," Glen said, "you should also know that Jim Rudolf, thirty-five-year-old astronaut, is our captain and head of the expedition. He is also a plumber and an electrician. His most important skill is his knowledge of mountain climbing. We will climb a lot on Mars."

Jim blinked his eyes and grinned. He stretched out longer than the others, all six and one half feet, floating.

"I have one other skill, Glen. Since you are 26, Mark is 20, and Wanda is 13, I'm an astronaut baby sitter." Wanda's laugh turned into a cough.

"Smoke!"

WANDA RELAXED, FLOATING LIKE A LEAF ON A POND.

Chapter Four
Asteroid or Moon?

"Smoke! Where is it coming from?" Wanda said. Mark swam to the super-conductive oven. Glen checked the air duct outlets. Jim pulled himself to the air intake vents.

"The intake vents are still closed," Jim said. They were supposed to be opened before we left the space station. I should have double-checked them. Here's one that's open. What is this?" He took a small object off of the protective screen and frowned. "Here's the culprit - a pill bottle." Wanda felt in her shirt pocket. Her pills – gone!

"My pills," she said. "I'm sorry. It's all my fault."

"We need to fix them so that won't happen again," Glen said. He took string from the tool bag and fastened the pill bottle around Wanda's neck. She tried not to spill her tears.

"Good thing you noticed that, Wanda. Our recycling system could have been hurt," Jim said, waving an electric ion cleaner to get rid of the smoke.

Wanda smiled. "I need another zippered bag, Glen, for my comb, gum and money." She grabbed a handful from her short's pocket. Glen dug another bag from the tool box. Then he and Jim checked the rest of the vents. They all relaxed, floating like leaves on a pond. Wanda put her bag of treasures in the pouch of her bed bag.

The dinner timer jingled. Wanda and Mark swam to the four doors of food. Wanda warmed the dinner trays in the super-conductive oven as Mark supervised.

"Good job, Wanda," he said. Wanda watched the others eat and tried to imitate them. She was careful to get her meatball in her mouth as she ate. She didn't want to see the marble-sized meatball floating in zero gravity, clogging a vent.

Six months later, Wanda was much better at holding on to little objects. She was looking forward to landing on Phobos, the moon of Mars. Her life on this spaceship was almost over. Wanda thought about her experiences as she looked out the window.

The first time I used the treadmill, I forgot how to stop it and get out of the box. I waved to Mark, who showed me the button that opened the rim and turned everything off. Wanda laughed to herself. *At least I did know what to do when I heard the siren that warned about another storm on the sun. I even beat the others to that little safe room. The sun's particles didn't seem to hurt anything.*

Wanda watched the nuclear engines spit out their plasma fire in the blackness of space. The small shiney engines balanced on the ends of four long pipes.

"The pipes send the plasma fuel to the engines," Glen said, "and keep the engines far enough from the ship to prevent it from catching on fire."

This stubby ship has engines sprouting from its top and a little Lander stuck to its back," Wanda said. "Our ship should be called 'Captured' instead of 'Freedom'. I like the way the pipes that hold the engines, turn. I get to see each engine that way. Oh, no! Glen, one engine isn't flashing fire!"

Glen swam through the ship to Jim. The two rushed back to Wanda's side. Jim watched through the round window. He studied the dead engine as it turned into view. Next Jim moved to the control panel and switched off all the engines. He and Glen put on suits, fastened tools and rope to their belts and left the ship through the airlock doors.

Mark put on ear phones and stood by the control panel. After a few minutes, Mark pulled the switch that started the engines rotating and spitting fire. Glen and Jim came back in.

"Wanda," Jim said, "thank you for calling this problem to our attention. The fuel hose to one engine came loose. Fuel was pouring into space instead of to the engine." Wanda looked into the blackness of space again with a frown on her face.

"Are we really moving?" she asked. "The star patterns don't look like they change."

"The ship does not turn as the planets do," Glen said, "so the stars don't seem to march across the sky."

The dinner bell sounded and Wanda followed Mark to the food chambers. After dinner, Wanda studied her Martian disks again. "When I go through these computer programs about Mars," Wanda told her brother. "I pretend that I'm on Mars, looking for the Face Rock in the Northern Hemisphere. Why do we have to go to the Southern Hemisphere? The programs have more information about the Northern Hemisphere of Mars. There's not much about the Southern Hemisphere."

"That's true," Glen said, "but Wanda, watch the programs while you walk on the treadmill. You need to exercise more. We're almost to the Martian moon, Phobos. Without more exercise, we'll have to carry you everywhere."

Wanda got into the box of the treadmill. Pushing button #1, caused the soft plastic rim of the box to slowly close around her waist. Button #2 instantly pulled out the air in the closed box. Her feet felt they were walking on solid ground as they moved the treadmill. Wanda walked another exercise hour while watching the Martian weather map program on the computer's LCD screen.

"There's something wrong with this treadmill, Glen. It's slowing down. I feel heavier all over." Glen nodded. *He's a big help,* Wanda thought as she kept walking. "Oh well, things break down. I won't be using it after we get to Phobos. Glen, it's hard to believe that Martian days are the same length as ours on Earth, but their seasons are twice as long."

"That's because Mars spins the same rate as Earth, to make our days, but being farther from the sun, the oval path Mars takes is twice as large as Earth's, making a longer year," Glen said, "and we'll be on Mars when it's mostly summer in the south."

Wanda decided to change to another part of the program, called 'Phobos'. She just had to call the program name to the computer.

"Phobos," Wanda said to the computer.

"Phobos," Mark called.

"Phobos," Glen said. "Wanda we're here. There's the little moon."

"As soon as we land on Phobos," Jim said, "we'll have to load our personal belongings in the Lander craft attached to our ship. Then we disconnect the Lander from the ship."

They brought their duffel bags and entered the Lander through a small round door in the back of the ship.

"Wanda," Glen said, "Put the computer back. Our station on Mars has computers." Wanda dragged it back, muttering.

"Just when I get used to it, I have to put it back. Those new computers are already three years old."

"This Lander, that fits onto the back of the spaceship, is an eight-foot, half-sphere," Glen said. They put on their suits and helmets and stepped out of the spaceship.

"Little rockets on the Lander's sides are like the folded legs of a fat spider," Wanda said. "The Lander looks like a soccer ball that's lost some of its air." Wanda looked down to see her feet hidden by dust. "I can walk on Phobos, like on the vacuum treadmill," Wanda said to the radio receiver in her helmet. "Now I know why I feel so heavy all over. The gravity of Phobos is pulling me, even though I can leap three feet just taking a step. Glen, the dust jumps up as I step, then falls down slowly."

Wanda practiced leaping about like the warrior heroes in Chinese films. One leap seemed to last too long, and Wanda was sitting in a hole. She only saw black sky and bouncing dust.

"Glen, I'm in a hole - a grave in three feet of dust!"

Chapter Five
Touchdown on Mars

"I WAS AFRAID your leaping would get you in trouble." Glen looked down at Wanda, sitting in three feet of fine silver dust. He reached out an arm. Wanda took Glen's hand and pulled him into the hole.

"Oh, sorry," Wanda said, pretending it was an accident. She felt herself picked up and thrown out of the hole, followed by a laughing brother.

"You do bounce nicely," he said, "but you're full of dust."

"Glen," Wanda said, laughing, "I feel like I'm dreaming – like I'm a tiny cricket, on a big dusty potato."

"Phobos is a potato-shaped asteroid, captured by Mars," Glen said. "Only thirteen miles wide, it hasn't enough gravity to hold together into a ball shape."

Wanda bounced over to where Jim and Mark were standing. Brushing the gray dust off her suit, Wanda said goodbye to their spaceship.

"My private room, computer and fun are being left behind." Wanda sighed. "I suddenly feel so alone."

"Others, coming from Mars, will take *Freedom* back to Earth," Jim said. "When we see that kind of ship again, two years will have gone by."

"When a ship like that returns," Glen said, "more people and supplies will be here." Mark carried his plastic maps.

"The ship will be larger," he said, "landing on Mars for us. After three years, I'll be ready to go back to Earth." Jim picked up a bundle of ropes and headed toward the Lander.

"Come on, Guys. It will only take a few hours for this moon to bring us over our jump point, so we'd better hurry and load the rest of our things in the Lander."

"I didn't think saying goodbye to the ship would be so hard," Glen said, tying down rumpled green duffel bags in the eight-foot Lander. Wanda took a last look at *Freedom* and the surface of Phobos, as she climbed into the Lander.

"Phobos is bare, but there are hills and craters," Wanda said as she buckled a harness across her chest. "Glittering silver dust covers everything. Only my shadow tells me the sun is shining on us. The sky is black with bright stars."

Wanda sat in one of six metal chairs, imbedded in the flat side of the Lander.

"These are crazy seats. I'm sitting in a hole." The oval back of the chair rose well above her head, sinking into the wall, about 3 inches. She sat between Glen and the door, while Mark sat on the other side of the door, next to Jim. Two extra seats between them, held duffel bags and bundles.

Across from the seats, a green oxygen tank was fastened to the curving wall. To its left was a blue water tank. Under these were more tied-down bundles.

"It's time to start the rockets," Jim said.

With the last seat buckles fastened, Jim pressed the buttons on the control panel next to him. Small rockets boosted the Lander from Phobos. The gentle lift-off surprised Wanda. She watched the dust settle down again on the small moon. The Lander sailed across the silver dust, to the other side of Phobos. The dust turned dark, in the shadows of Phobos' night.

Now Wanda could see Mars. The red planet, sparkling in the sun, filled the sky. It was so close that Wanda could not see the North or South poles. The astronauts were hurling upward.

Jim pushed three buttons again, turning off three rockets.

"We turn into the atmosphere of Mars slowly," Jim said. When the turn was complete, Jim shut off the fourth rocket. Another button caused metal shields to cover each side.

"Won't we crash without rockets?" Wanda asked as her eyes tried to adjust to the dim light.

"We are now orbiting into the atmosphere sideways," Jim said, "slowing down our approach with friction. We don't want to reach the surface too soon. It's called aerobraking."

"These window covers protect us from the heat caused by the friction, Wanda," Glen said. "Friction makes your hands hot when you rub them together."

Glen has to think he's teaching me something I don't know, Wanda thought, smiling to herself. Wanda felt Mars gravity pulling her back into her metal seat.

"The thick air puts friction on space ships, but also meteorites coming to the planet's surface," Glen said. "Fiery meteorites are what we call 'shooting stars.'"

Jim reversed the rockets to slow the Lander as they dropped through the air of Mars. A jerk let them know the rockets were slowing their fall. Another jerk and a swaying motion made Jim open the metal covers.

"The parachutes are doing their job," Jim said, looking up through the window, "It's a shame this Lander isn't any use after we hit ground."

"Yes," Glen said, "the motor was only made for one landing."

Watching the Marineris Valley, to the north, open wider, Jim nodded to Mark.

"Mark, your calculations brought us to the right spot."

"Isn't that the largest valley in our solar system?" Wanda asked, "and underneath us, isn't that the Hellas Plains - the brightest spot on Mars, seen from Earth telescopes?" Wanda smiled at Glen's surprised look at her. She whispered to Mark, "Thanks to you, I beat Glen to the punch."

"That's right, Wanda," Glen said. "This is the Hellas crater, full of softer soil. It has fewer visible craters inside its rim. That's the reason our station was dropped here. Mr. Llyons of Llyons Aircraft, sent the station to Mars for us, three years ago. He felt the Hellas Plains would be the safest place to land. Southern Mars is choked with craters, every where else."

They floated down, a silver, half-sphere Lander, held up by three parachutes. The swaying trip ended in a jolting thud, as they hit the orangish ground of Mars. Wanda got out of her chair, feeling the heavy pull of Mars.

"My head aches – but at least it is not a migraine."

"Here's my map," Mark said. "We still have a few more miles before we reach Mars Station #2."

They unloaded four duffel bags. Glen and Jim folded red-striped parachutes.

"We may need this nice material," Glen said.

"For curtains?" Wanda asked, "or my dress?"

"My ropes and the bags of lichens can stay here," Jim said. "But we'll have to make another trip back to the Lander for six boxes of tomato and lettuce plants."

"We don't want anything to happen to those plants now," Mark said, "after Wanda took such good care of them."

Wanda kicked into a soft hill where the wind had pushed fine sand.

"That's a little sand dune," Glen said. "There are a lot of them in these southern craters."

"This sand dune reminds me of snow on Earth," Wanda said. Of course, Earth snow wouldn't have little snowballs all over – like those little dusty rocks. Too bad we don't have sleds."

"Great idea, Wanda," Jim said. "We can bring everything with us. I'll get the window shields. They'll make good sleds."

The men cut off metal shields that now hung like folded wings on the sides of the Lander. They piled the rest of the boxes on them. With a few of Jim's ropes, Glen and Jim began pulling their sleds over sand dunes and potato-sized rocks. Mark carried the duffel bags.

Wanda looked down at her boots, dusty with the orangish Martian dirt. Tiny, glittering triangles danced over the boots in a large semi-circle.

"Glen, I'm getting a migraine."

Chapter Six
Station #2 Awaits

"We have to stop!" Glen said. He hurried with Wanda back to the Lander. Shutting the door, he turned on the oxygen in the green can. When the spot on his sleeve turned green, Glen took off his helmet.

"That color change lets us know when there's enough oxygen to breathe. Can you reach your migraine pills?"

Wanda removed her helmet and pushed her hand into her suit. She found her pills, popped one in her mouth and drank the water that Glen gave her from the blue water tank. Fastening their helmets, they returned to the others.

"Sorry, Glen."

"Don't be silly." He carried the blue and green tanks out with them. "I'm glad you told us while we were this close to the Lander. Let me rearrange these sleds." Glen piled all the boxes on one sled and Wanda onto the other. Mark carried four duffel bags.

Glen is just as good at babying me as Mom was, Wanda thought. *I'm sure I could walk, since I took the pill right away. If Glen keeps me in bed, every time I get a migraine, I won't have any fun on Mars.* Wanda felt her sled screech to a stop.

"We have to stop again," Glen said. "See that yellow fog? It's a dust storm!"

The four space travelers huddled together, holding boxes over their heads as dust and sand whirled about them.

"You'll be alright, Wanda," Glen said. "I'll keep the sharp sand from your visor. If the helmets are too scratched we'll have a hard time seeing." After about an hour, the wind slowed and dropped the last of its dust.

"Now which way do we go?" Jim asked. "The dust storm has hidden our footprints."

"Well," Mark said, "the sun is not much help. It seems to be slightly west or south. I don't know which."

"I can barely see the Lander," Glen said, "but is it east or south?"

"If we put together, what we know about the sun and the Lander," Wanda said, "the Lander would be southeast and the sun would be southwest. So I think we should go north." Wanda pointed to the direction she thought was north.

"Jim," Glen said, "don't you have your finder? The station has a directional signal. It is supposed to be activated by your finder." Jim took a small black box out of his pouch and pressed a button on it.

"We go that way." Jim pointed north, in the same direction Wanda pointed. "These homing devices are important on a planet with little magnetic force."

"I'm glad Mr. Llyons thought to equip the station with a homing device," Glen said. "A radio signal from Jim's remote control box turns the homing device on in the station."

"But Jim," Mark said, "if you forget your finder we can always use Wanda." Wanda grinned.

They tramped onward for about two more hours, singing to the tune of "Row, row, row your boat, "Wanda, Wanda, show us the way".

"There's the station!" Wanda said. The round metal building had a silvery-pink shine in the late afternoon sun. The station was half buried in sandy, Martian soil.

"Its upper parts are covered with solar panels," Glen said. "They provide energy for heat and electricity."

"We need to dig out a path." Jim said, unpacking the shovels from his duffel bag.

The astronauts dug their path through a foot of fine orangish dust, to the door of the Station.

"At least this door opens inward," Glen said. "That's an improvement over the old station. On my last trip, we had to replace its outward-opening door after a boulder held the door shut." Glen entered the door and closed it again when everyone was in the small area.

"Normally, when we go through this next door, we can take off our helmets," Glen said, "but this time, we have to turn on the oxygen first. Once started, the station has a good recycling system for both air and water."

The astronauts passed through the inner door.

"This station is just the way you described it," Jim said. "I feel like I've been here before."

"Mr. Llyons told me it's like the one we had fifteen years ago in the Northern Hemisphere. That one is now being used by Headquarters and the Gardener's Group, here on Mars."

"How did they get this two-room house to sit down without being on a tilt?" Wanda asked her brother.

"This two-room house has remote-controlled rockets that helped the station land. The rockets turned sideways, after landing, letting the station spin slowly. Twisting into the soft ground of this great crater, the station buried its heat shield and rockets."

They wandered inside the station, looking at the piles of frozen foods and tied bundles of furniture parts.

"This is our station - home for two years," Jim said. "We must get the frozen food and those pipes outside, before we turn on the oxygen. It's too crowded in here, now, to put the furniture together."

"What are those pipes used for?" Wanda asked, looking at a bundle of nine-foot, metal pipes along the inner wall.

"We push the pipes into the ground where we expect to find water," Jim said. "They are made of the new space-age metal that is stronger than steel and lighter than aluminum."

"How do you get those pipes in the ground?" Wanda asked.

"We have a machine that pushes them down like screws into wood. We'll have to find that machine. Wanda, will you hold the inner door of the air lock open? Mark, hold the outer door. Glen and I will get these pipes out of the way."

After the pipes were out of the station, the men carried out boxes of frozen food. Wanda looked over the station. The front room, loaded with supplies, had green walls. Through the central doorway was a second room, with yellow walls. The green room was full of food boxes and bundles of furniture parts. On the side of the archway between the two big rooms was a door – the only door for the inner house.

Chapter Seven
Oven for Dirt

WANDA OPENED THE door of a small white room, to find -- *The bathroom! With a tub, a sink, and ... that looks like a washer and dryer. There's a toilet on the other side.* She left the bathroom, to find a tiny room with only three walls. *That is called a cubical,* Wanda thought, *with a three-foot-wide silver radio.* Mark came to her side.

"Isn't that a great radio, Wanda?" He sat down and plugged the radio into his helmet.

Wanda heard the men's voices in her helmet. She threaded her way through the piles of boxes and a two-foot square machine.

That machine has a big hole in its center. I know it's a machine because it's metal and has switches, she thought. Wanda heard Jim's voice.

"Now we can look for the machine that goes with those pipes." Wanda found Jim and Glen searching through bundles and boxes.

"How can those pipes help you find water?" Wanda asked. "One pipe has a point on it, and they're all decorated with ripples."

"You have sharp eyes, Wanda," Jim said. "The pipes are threaded on the outside. Those are the ripples you saw. The machine we're looking for, is also threaded in a central hole. It uses the threads to push those pipes into the ground, like a giant screw driver. The pipe with the point goes first and the rest are screwed on as they go down, to make one ninety-foot pipe. When the pipe reaches water, the water shoots up and out its top."

"Just like the oil wells I read about," Wanda said. "Jim, I found a machine with a hole." Wanda motioned to the men to follow her. "Is this what you're looking for?"

"This is the very thing we are looking for," Jim said, "a machine that pushes water pipes into the ground. You do have sharp eyes, Wanda."

"Thanks, Little Sister." Glen took the machine outside. "I can take the frozen food outside, Jim," Wanda said, picking up food boxes, "but before I go, I want to know how you make that machine work. Do you have a long electric cord?"

"The machine has a rechargeable battery. Before we use it, we charge the battery overnight by hooking it to the station's electrical outlet." Wanda carried her packages outside. Mark joined her with more food packages.

"I told Headquarters that we got here," Mark said. "Jim, we have most of the food outside."

"Good. I'll push this first button, to heat the water pipes and thaw our water," Jim said, walking over to the wall control panel. "I'll wait to turn on our room heat until you tell me all the frozen food is outside."

"I'll look for our super-conductive oven," Mark said, "and start fixing dinner."

"We need to find that solar oven, too," Glen said.

"I made a solar oven when I was a Boy Scout," Mark said as he looked for his cooker in the piles of furniture parts. "We just used a shiny piece of thin metal, bent in a semi-circle and set into a wooden frame. The metal threw strong sunlight to a central area, where we held a hot dog on a stick to cook."

"Ours is an outdoor oven, used for cooking soil," Glen said. "The soil releases oxygen and water."

"Our solar oven is complicated," Jim said, "and large. It has tanks for storing both water and oxygen. The Solar Oven is a machine, using solar energy to move along the ground scraping up permafrost. We'll have to find a good area and remove surface stones, to use it."

"Will we use its water for cooking?" Wanda asked.

"No, for washing," Glen said. "But we could drink it if we have to. It's like drinking rusty water. I once tried it with some instant coffee. The coffee turned green and tasted awful."

"If we boil the water and let it condense," Mark said, "we can purify it the same way moisture clings to the outside of a cold glass."

"I made a Science Fair Project showing water evaporation," Wanda said. "The salt in the saltwater stayed in the glass when the water evaporated. Will the iron be left behind like the salt?"

"Yes, that's how our recycling system works," Glen said. "We'll get rusty water into the recycling system as we use that water for washing. We don't want to put too much rust in at once and clog the machinery."

Wanda watched Jim assemble the table and bunk beds from aluminum and plastic legs and planks.

"We have more bunk beds than we need," Jim said. "Wanda, will you put these bundles in the corner? We'll need beds if more people come."

"Who will be coming besides my teacher?" Wanda asked.

"Other astronauts are planning to come here," Jim said. Glen and Wanda carried more frozen food packages out and placed them in the shadow of the station's south side.

"Do we stack food on the south side because of the shadow?" Wanda asked.

"That and because we're near the equator. This is only temporary until we assemble plastic bins for the food. In summer, the temperature gets up to 45 degrees near our heads in the sun. In the shade and near the ground, it's still below freezing."

"Headquarters radioed that our next shipment from Earth is coming in a few months," Mark said. "I'm expecting fresher food."

"And my pills," Wanda said. "I hope Mom sends clothes. I had to rinse mine out every night on the ship. I just wore them in the shower." She laughed. "Good thing that shower came with a dryer, too."

"So that's what took you so long every night," Glen said, laughing. "Wanda, since you are an expert clothes washer, you can man the washer and dryer in our bathroom. We have a pile of dirty clothes in our duffel bags." Wanda stuck out her tongue at her brother.

When the last food package was out of the station, the doors were closed. Jim turned on the heat and oxygen. The color-spots on their sleeves soon turned green. Everyone took off their helmets and suits.

"I'll turn on the water recycling system," Jim said. "when the signal sounds that the water has thawed. I'll just leave on the heat for the hot water pipes."

Ten minutes later, while they were fitting the furniture parts together, a buzzer rang. Jim moved the switch.

"Stop," Mark called, "we have a leak!"

"Mark, I never made bread in any kind of oven, but don't tell."

Chapter Eight
Repairs First

Jim pushed the handle back again, turning off the water. He looked at the wet area.

"This heavy plastic pipe looks like it was split when installed. I think my silver duct tape will solve the problem." Jim rummaged around in his tool box. "It's not here!"

"I know where it is," Wanda said. "You used it in the Lander to keep the duffel bags from falling on us when the Lander turned sideways."

"Right," Mark said. "Will my hospital tape work?"

"It might," Jim said, "if we use enough of it." Jim wrapped the white tape around the white plastic pipe.

"The white tape looks better than silver duct tape," Wanda said, "since our pipes are white."

"Here's the test," Jim said. He turned the water handle once more. When no water spouted out of the taped place, everyone cheered.

"Thanks, Wanda," Jim said, "for remembering about the duct tape. I'd still be looking for it."

Wanda smiled and glanced out the round window.

"Dust storm!" She called. The station sounded like loud static as the small rocks hit its metal sides.

"Wow," Mark said, "do many of these dust storms happen on Mars?"

"Yes," Glen said. "That's the trouble with southern Martian summers. Sometimes dust storms last all day."

"I hope they won't all last as long as that," Jim said. "Temperatures get colder as dusty air reflects the sun and keeps the heat from the surface of Mars. But at night, the temperature is higher than its usual minus 150 degrees. The dust holds in what little heat does radiate from Mars. Good thing we have solar batteries for the station. They store the electricity we need when our solar panels can't work."

"I can't fix the dinner tonight," Mark said. "I'm sorry. Our super-conductive oven is not working."

"I'll have to take the oven apart, to fix it," Jim said.

"I can help you, Mark," Wanda said, "Before we left the space ship, I stuck nuts and dried apricots in my duffel bag."

"Thanks," Mark said. "That's better than nothing."

"Remember, we also have tomatoes." Wanda put the finger foods in the center of the table. "I'm glad we can just pick the tomatoes now." Everyone began to eat.

"Wow, my taster is working again. This is the best food I tasted since we left Earth!"

"Yes," Mark said, "I told you we would be able to taste again, after we landed on Mars." Mark gave Wanda a smile. "Jim, I radioed Station #1. The woman teacher is due in a month."

It's not fair, Wanda thought, *They find water and I study. I hope that new teacher isn't a grouch.*

"The wind has died down." Glen said. "At least we'll be able to sleep."

Wanda wiped the plastic table top with a damp piece of the red and white parachute.

"This material is so pretty, I could make a robe out of it. Glen, could we get needles and thread in the next supplies?"

"Mark can ask our new member to bring some," Glen said, pumping the air mattresses.

Mark soon had the table full of his maps and the solar convection oven for Jim to fix. Glen set up Wanda's bed in the yellow room with the food plants. He used some of the red and white parachute cloth for privacy. Wanda liked the way the cloth hung down from the ceiling with an overlapping "doorway". Now the yellow room was divided in half.

"Here you are, Wanda," Glen put an armload of dirty clothes in the little bathroom. Wanda stuck her tongue out at him.

Mom always put colored clothes in cold water, white cottons in hot water, and the rest in warm water. Wanda said to herself. *But I'll put them all in cold water to conserve our hot water for my bath.* She giggled to herself. *Being the first one to take a bath, is the perk of doing the wash.*

Wanda left the bathroom an hour later with wet hair and an armload of clean clothes. Glen was pulling a three-foot high machine out of her room.

"I found the solar oven," Glen said. "It was in the corner, hidden by what looks like a pile of sheets and covers."

"Covers - just what we need for a good night's sleep," Jim said. "Mark, I fixed the oven. A wire just came loose – probably when the station landed here. We get up at dawn, people. Tomorrow we look for water."

Wanda was excited as she crawled into her bed covers. She drifted off to sleep, dreaming about pushing pipes into the ground for water. *Wanda watched as the men drove pipes into the ground. Then the crater began to shrink. She was alone. The pipes jumped up and pushed themselves through the machine, into the ground. Water squirted out of the last pipe.*

Wanda woke with a start. She thought about her dream. *If you give no thought about what you do,* her father always said, *you will have no memory of it.* Wanda knew he was talking about leaving keys without thinking, then not knowing where they were. *I always thought his words were true about dreams, too. If I didn't think about a dream as soon as I woke, I wouldn't remember it.* Wanda's eyes opened wide. She smiled to herself.

"If I look in smaller craters, like I did in my dream, maybe I'll find water all by myself!" Wanda said to the wall.

Next morning, Wanda woke to hear Jim and Glen talking.

"NASA is sure this Niesten Crater has water under an icy crust," Jim said. "We can walk there and back in a day. It's just by the northern rim of our Hellas Crater."

"You and I can," Glen said. "Let's leave Wanda here with Mark. He can mind the radio and help Wanda with cooking."

"I hope you don't find water," Wanda muttered.

Wanda woke to find herself in a spotlight. The Martian sun washed over her bed. *I'll have to make curtains for that window,* she thought. She took off her nightgown that used to be Glen's shirt. Pulling on her worn blue shirt and navy shorts, she found she was hungry. Parting her parachute doorway, Wanda saw Mark at the radio with his earphones on. She tapped Mark on the shoulder. He looked up from the radio and took off his ear-phones.

"Well, you got up! You needed the sleep after that bad migraine yesterday. Sorry I can't help with migraines. If you break a leg or anything, as health official, I can help you."

"Thanks. I think I'll break an arm instead of a leg. That way, I can go places but have less work to do." Mark laughed.

"I can help you prevent migraines – with tranquilizers, or give you sleeping pills after you have one." Mark smiled. "I saved your scrambled eggs. Just heat them for 20 seconds in the super-conductive oven. Jim got it fixed last night." Wanda got her breakfast.

"Mark, these are the best eggs I've had in a year!"

"Thanks. I put out the things you need for making bread. If you want anything else, let me know." Wanda sat with her mouth open. "Wanda, what's the matter?"

"I never made bread in your kind of oven," Wanda whispered. "Mark, I never made bread in any kind of oven, but don't tell."

"Don't worry," Mark said, laughing. "I'll teach you right now. I have a secret too. I'm not 20, I'm 18 years old. Shall we be partners in crime?" Wanda laughed.

"Why did you say you were twenty?"

"I was afraid Jim would want an older member in his crew."

When Wanda finished eating, Mark showed her how to mix the flour, sugar, powdered eggs, powdered milk, water and his important yeast. The dough was covered in the bowl, to sit for half an hour. Then Wanda divided the dough into balls. Mark showed her how to knead the dough. She pushed it on the flour dusted tabletop. Each ball of dough was baked in their oven. Wanda sank into a chair as the last little loaf was baked.

"Mark, I can't wait. It smells so good!" Wanda and Mark munched the last little ball of crusty bread.

Hours later, Jim and Glen returned for chunky beef stew smelling of onions and bay leaf with crusty loaves of bread.

"No luck, finding water in Niesten crater," Jim said. "NASA will be disappointed. Their photos showed signs of water."

"We did see the effects of water erosion on the snowy ridges of Niesten Crater," Glen said. "Water may still be in the depths of the crater and we just can't reach it. With such a large crater, water could be a mile down. Our pipes only go down ninety feet."

"Tomorrow, we'll look in a crater near-by, to the west," Jim said, "inside our Hellas Crater."

Why do I feel guilty, Wanda asked herself, *just because I wished they would fail?*

Jim and Glen joined together, four plastic bins. Mark and Wanda spent the rest of the day, sorting the frozen foods. They put meat in the first bin, vegetables in the second, fruit and deserts in the third and cooking supplies in the fourth.

For another month, the men searched for water in nearby craters. Jim reported to NASA, the failure to find water.

"At least the solar oven works, rolling over icy permafrost," Jim told NASA. He was about to turn off the radio when a message came from Headquarters at Station #1.

"Wanda," Jim called, "your teacher is on her way. Our fifth member should be here sometime today. She will be driving a rover." Jim handed the earphones to Mark.

"Jim," Mark called from the radio, "I just received two more messages from the director at Station #1. A Chinese team is on its way to Mars, to join the gardeners there. Director Jake Hampton also wants us to know that Mars is entering a group of meteorites in its orbit. He will be scanning the heavens for the next few weeks."

Wanda watched out the window for her new teacher as she studied her laptop computer. After about half an hour, Wanda jumped up.

"Oh, I see that yellowish fog. It's another dust storm!"

Pat Davis

"I'm a real Martian," Julia said, winking a hazel eye, "with hair to match Mars soil."

Chapter Nine
Julia Joins

Glen hurried to the window to see the oncoming dust storm. He laughed.

"Wanda, that isn't a dust storm," Glen said, that's your new teacher. She's supposed to be bringing your Migraine pills and Mark's fresh food from the Earth space ship that came last week. She's making her own little dust storm."

The astronauts were about to go outside when the new teacher entered the station.

"Hello, boys and girl," the dusty astronaut said, "I have packages for you on top of my rover. The spaceship from Earth brought them when my crew headed for home. Name's Julia."

Wanda's group passed through the double doors of the air lock with the new teacher and carried back boxes and triangular-shaped packages. Wanda slipped out of her space suit and waited. Mark stepped in front of Wanda and frowned at her.

"Wanda, what are you doing?" Before she could answer, he wiped the red jelly off of her mouth.

"Mark, I didn't want the new teacher to know I was a kid," she whispered. "I didn't have lipstick, so I used the next best thing." Mark's laugh was quieted by his own right hand. His left hand held Wanda's arm.

Julia removed her helmet, freeing a mop of wavy red hair and a big smile.

"I'm a real Martian," she said, winking a hazel eye, "with hair to match Mars soil." She looked at Wanda. "I thought I'd be taking care of a little boy. Instead, I see a big girl - and you are Wanda." She gave Wanda a hug. Wanda couldn't help smiling, in spite of herself.

After introductions, the men opened packages like kids on Christmas morning. Mark picked up a small package and held it out to Wanda.

"Here are your migraine pills, Wanda." Mark shuffled packages wrapped in heavy plastic. "This must be the frozen chickens and vegetables in these lumpy packages. They are well frozen, Julia. It was smart of you to have them tied to the roof of your Van." Julia smiled, as Glen grabbed a soft package.

"Oh, this must be a package for you, Wanda," Glen said. "Sorry I opened it. Looks like your clothes."

"Thanks, Glen," Wanda said, blushing. *Underwear! Why did Glen have to open it? Mom sent me underwear!*

"What is this big triangular-shaped package?" Mark said.

"Not your food," Glen said, laughing, as metal parts and wheels fell out when Mark opened it. "These pieces look like parts to a little car - a rover!"

"That's what it is," Jim said, holding up a yard-wide sheet of directions for putting a little rover together. "We can assemble it tomorrow, after we check out those large craters to the north, for water. Julia, may we use your Van? You and Wanda can stay here and get to know each other better."

"Come on, the dinner's waiting," Wanda said. *Why can't the men ever take me to find water?* Wanda smiled as she watched her brother pull out a chair for Julia.

Wanda' smile turned into a frown, as Glen and Julia had a private conversation. *Glen is really being silly around Julia,* she thought. *He never pulled out a chair for me, and now he's whispering with her.* Wanda pretended she didn't notice.

Wanda began passing the roast beef with vegetables.

"I cooked these myself," she told Julia.

"I thought I'd be teaching you, but you'll be teaching me as well. There is a lot I need to learn about cooking."

Julia is the perfect friend, Wanda thought, smiling, *I found a sister - a pretend sister.*

The men gulped their food in a rush, stopping between bites to stare at the map of Mars, they had positioned between them.

"Julia, they can't wait to drive your Van to the northern craters." Wanda's lower lip dragged the floor.

"This is very good roast beef you made, Wanda," Julia said in a loud voice, so the men could hear her. The men's eyes opened in surprise. Wanda smiled at the sudden notice the men gave to Julia's words.

"Very nice meal," Glen and Jim agreed. Mark nodded at Wanda and smiled. Wanda couldn't help grinning with Julia, as the men left, waving to the girls.

"Well," Wanda said to Julia, as they stood alone in the station, "You came a long way, and I'm sure you're tired. Do you want to take a bath while I wash the dishes?"

"You just read my mind," Julia said. Wanda picked up towels and soap to hand to Julia. Julia laid them on the table and motioned for Wanda to sit down beside her.

"Wanda, I need to tell you something. Your brother is concerned about you. He asked me to talk to you about female problems."

"That's what he was whispering to you before we ate? Julia, both my mother and grandmother told me all about the birds and the bees when I was in second grade!"

"I'm sure they did," Julia said. "Glen wants me to talk to you about your recent problems."

"My brother – I guess he does love me. That explains why he didn't fuss with me about staying in the shower so long, and taking more than one bath a day."

"I have a product to give you," Julia said. She opened a small box she was holding. "This little sponge-cup can be rinsed out and used again, right away."

"Thanks, Julia."

"At first this was invented to help women on space ships or in war," Julia said. "But our world is changing. Our 'throw-away society' is giving way to a more conservative place where everyone is aware of recycling and saving the trees."

"You are right, Julia. Thanks again. I should have known that even though I was going to Mars, I am still becoming a woman. Your product is much appreciated. I'm glad you have a pamphlet to go with it. I need all the instruction I can get." Wanda laughed and gave Julia a kiss on the cheek, before going to wash the dishes.

Julia took her soap and towel to the bathroom. An hour later, Julia was refreshed and dressed in blue-green shorts and shirt that contrasted her orange-red hair. Julia unpacked her box of disks for the computer.

"Wanda, would you help me look over these disks?" she asked. "We can save the easier ones for younger kids."

"Yes," Wanda said. "I just finished putting the chicken stew in the oven." The girls grouped the disks into special piles.

"Math, Science and Home Economics," Julia named the piles. "That last one is for me," she said, laughing.

"Let's start with the first math test," Wanda said. "I'm good at math." Wanda smiled as the test proved her right. The girls spent the next few hours going over the material together. They soon weeded out other disks that were too easy.

Wanda took a break from her work, to check on her chicken stew and brew some tea. She glanced out the window.

"It's getting dark, Julia. The men aren't here yet. Could they have had trouble with your Van?" The girls stared out the window together.

"Look, here they come," Julia said.

The men entered the room and tore off their helmets. Wanda could tell that they had more bad luck.

"Boys," Julia said, "you'll have plenty of time to check out more craters. Wanda spent a lot of time and energy making this great dinner for you." Wanda smiled. *Julia is just the friend I need.*

After Wanda's chicken stew was gobbled, the men seemed to be in better spirits. Mark washed the dishes while Jim and Glen read the directions for making the rover. The girls played a computer game. Then everyone went to bed. Wanda climbed up to sleep on the new top bunk as Julia snored in the lower one.

I always wanted an upper bunk. Julia must have really been tired. She's sound asleep. Wanda woke up in the night, to use the bathroom. Her first step out of bed was a surprise. She landed on the floor, with a crash.

"Wanda!" Julia found her on the floor. "Are you hurt?"

Chapter Ten
Trial Run

Wanda picked herself up off the floor.

"I'm just bruised, I think. I forgot I was on the top bunk."

"You're lucky you did this on Mars with its lower gravity. On Earth, you would have a broken leg. You take my bed." Julia climbed to the top bunk. "I'm used to upper bunks."

"Thanks, Julia," Wanda limped to the bathroom. She put a cold washcloth on her bruised legs. Then she splashed water on her hot face. *Mark will think I'm trying to break something so he can help me. I know he'll want to practice his medical skills. I won't tell him.*

Wanda crawled into the lower bunk but was too excited to sleep. She watched the sun rise, melting the frost into a bluish water vapor. Soon the vapor was lost in the orange dust of the Martian air. Now the sky had its pink color, as Wanda crept out of bed and into a fresh pair of blue-jeans and a yellow knit blouse.

"I'll fix breakfast before Mark gets up," she said to herself. "Nobody will know about my silly accident." She put the powdered eggs and flour that Mark had measured out, into a bowl. Then she mixed in water, to make flat pancakes. After baking in the oven, they were filled with the sugared peaches Mark had fixed the night before. Wanda was folding the pancakes around the peaches, into little tortillas, when she felt a touch on her shoulder.

"So," Julia whispered, "You're making a surprise breakfast. I'll make the coffee." Wanda smiled.

When the men awoke, breakfast was on the table.

"These are good," Glen said, "and delicate. Wanda," Glen lowered his voice. "I heard something fall last night. Is Julia alright?"

"Julia is fine. I just stumbled," Wanda whispered. *I don't know whether to kiss him or kick him*, She thought.

As soon as breakfast was over, the girls cleared the table and Jim dismantled it. The men put the rover parts on the floor and studied the directions for putting it together.

Wanda and Julia listened to them as they did the dishes.

"By the picture, it's an open rover," Glen said. "We'll have to keep on our suits when we ride in it. There's room for a few oxygen tanks in the back seat."

"After we get the car together," Jim said, "we have to practice driving it." Then they spread out the car parts on the floor.

Under Jim's guidance, Mark and Glen connected the parts of the little car. It was beginning to look like a machine, but in four pieces.

"We can take these parts out of the station to finish putting them together," Jim said. The men assembled the table again. Wanda and Julia immediately covered the table with disks to study on Wanda's computer. Two hours later, the men entered the station and removed their helmets.

"How will we get the thing to run?" Glen asked.

"You put on the solar panel, didn't you?" Jim asked. "Just give the sun time to charge its batteries. It's a simple machine that doesn't have the strong 2,000 mAh batteries in Julia's Van. Those weak 300 mAh batteries keep this little car moving in sunlight, but not in the dark."

"It looks like a bucket with over-grown wheels." Mark said.

"A green bucket with a loose lid," Glen said.

"The lid is the solar panel," Jim said. The men started for the door to take turns driving the "Bucket". "Girls, we promise to be back by nightfall."

Wanda and Julia smiled.

"Julia, I'll be surprised if they come back before dark."

"I have a good idea," Julia said. "Let's take this opportunity to radio Earth. We could tell your parents how things are going."

"That's a great idea, Julia. But Mark always got the messages off to them, before." Julia smiled.

"I know how to do it, Wanda. But first, we have to write down what we want to say to them. I get jittery and forget what I want to say to someone on Earth, if I don't write it down."

After half an hour of deciding what to say, Julia and Wanda talked to the Rolands. Between sending their messages and waiting half-an hour for the answers, the afternoon was gone.

"I knew the men should have taken my rover, too. It will move in the dark." Wanda peered out the round window.

"I see waving lights!" Wanda said, "flashlights! They are here!" Three astronauts straggled into the station and sank into chairs.

"At least when our "Bucket" runs out of solar energy," Glen said, "we can pick it up and carry it."

"I wish we carried the "Bucket" a shorter distance," Mark said. "I'm worn out."

"Well," Glen said, "You were the one who wanted to go just a little farther before we turned around."

"Mark, you just didn't want to cook dinner," Wanda said, laughing. "Don't worry, you don't have to cook, Mark. Julia and I made dinner. Tomorrow we'll practice driving the bucket while all of you rest." Julia smiled and nodded.

Next morning, eating Mark's breakfast of eggs and toast, Julia and Wanda made plans to drive the "Bucket." Jim showed them the diagram of the controls.

Wanda and Julia pulled on their suits and left to drive the four-foot square "Bucket." Julia practiced first, discovering how to drive the green box-like car with its reflective solar- paneled roof. The wheels were wide, and rode over small boulders without any trouble.

Wanda watched Julia's handling of the wheel and buttons, then switched seats with her. Pushing a button to move the "Bucket," she jerked forward, again and again.

"Julia, what am I doing wrong?" Julia reached over and pushed the auto-leveling button. Now the car ran slower, but more smoothly.

"Thanks, Julia. Oh, there's a big boulder." Wanda turned the "Bucket" around the foot-high boulder, and almost turned it over.

"Don't worry," Julia said. "I heard Jim say: 'This baby will be hard to overturn.' The wheels are big, but the body of this little car is close to the ground. I can see how this rover is easy to drive on the smoother Hellas Plains, but not too good for rougher places, like Chryse Plains where Viking 1 stands."

After an hour of switching places, with starts and stops, the girls were laughing about their crazy driving as they returned to the station.

They found the men sitting around the table, looking at Mark's heavy plastic map of Southern Mars.

"You came back just in time," Glen said. "We want to look for water in Barnard Crater." Mark used a grease pencil to show their path on the map.

"We will travel due south, to the southern edge of Hellas Plains and cross the oval-shaped Amphitrites Crater to Barnard Crater. That's about 500 miles. If we travel in the "Bucket", at 25 miles an hour, we will take about four days."

"We'll pick up the *"Lander"*, on the way," Jim said. "Our useless Lander will make a good mobile house."

"Wanda, you and Julia can work on your studies while we are gone," Glen said.

"But we want to go with you," Julia said. "Wanda should see you get water. We can always study computer disks." Wanda was biting her lip. "Wanda and I could drive my Van to pull the Lander." Julia added. "My Van has a solar battery that holds a charge of 2,000 mAh. We can drive the van in the dark, if we need to. We could get there in half the time. The van could easily go 50 miles an hour on this smooth plain."

"Good idea," Glen said, looking a little sheepish.

"At least you can get Glen to change his mind," Wanda whispered to Julia as she hurried to get ready.

A twenty-minute, ride to the south brought the Van to an eight foot half-sphere laying at a tilt in the red dust.

"That must be the Lander," Julia said.

"Your lichens are inside the Lander too, Glen," Jim said, removing some ropes from the Lander. "We will have a chance to plant lichens as we return to the station. Fasten these ropes to the Lander's dead rockets, then tie them to the Van."

"Wow," Wanda said, "I'm glad the Lander wasn't any farther away, Julia. I'm sure that sitting on your lap put your legs to sleep." Julia laughed as she helped Glen and Mark drag the "Bucket" out of the Van. Wanda brought out the four extra wheels to put under the Lander.

"The Lander isn't very heavy," Mark said, as he and Glen fastened wheels under it. Last, the men fastened the "Bucket" behind the Lander with a metal rod that had a closable hook on each end.

"That rod will keep the "Bucket" from banging into the back of the *"Lander",*" Jim said, laughing, "unless it goes sideways."

For two hours, Wanda saw rippling sand dunes as they reached the center of the gigantic bowl of Hellas Plains.

"The biggest sand box on Mars, and I can't play in it," Wanda said, laughing. "I see craters! Mark, you said there were no craters on the Hellas Plains."

"Those craters are on the edge of the Hellas Plains. Besides, they are too small to bother with. We're more likely to find water in a big crater like Barnard." Wanda pictured herself in the "Bucket", riding around in the small craters.

"Why do you have to find water in big craters?" Wanda asked as they rode past the group of small craters on the way to large Barnard Crater.

"We think big craters have large, deep bodies of water," Glen said, "but we could plant lichens in these small craters. Lichens will live nicely on the large, flat rocks inside the craters and help put oxygen on Mars."

"I read that these rocks are carbonate and hold some of the early atmosphere of Mars," Wanda said.

"Some rocks are," Jim said, "these rocks are formed from water. They are limestone. If you look closely, you will see tiny balls of grey hematite. NASA scientists were thrilled when the little balls were discovered, back in 2007. NASA scientists called them Blueberries. Hematite is the proof that Mars had water at one time. Hematite is a type of iron-ore that forms in water. "

The caravan once again, was traveling up and down the sand dunes. Mark watched the sun through a five-inch, silver tube.

"Is that a telescope," Wanda asked.

"No, Wanda, it's a directional finder to make sure we follow the path to the south. This instrument will keep us from riding around in circles."

Even going 50 miles an hour, they were still within the Hellas Plains at sun set, traveling upward to its rim.

"Winds have blown sand dunes across the boundary of the Hellas Plains," Mark said, "making the south end of the plains hard to see on my map. We will know when we get to the rim, by the way the land suddenly flattens and we are no longer going uphill. By tomorrow noon, we should come to Barnard Crater." They stopped with the setting sun and Mark handed out the cheese tortillas. Wanda gave out drinks. After supper, the girls slept in the folded Van seats and the men stretched out in the Lander.

Traveling up and down rocky hills, next day, brought them to an unexpected sight.

"Ice!" Jim said. Before them stretched an ice field, as large as a small crater.

Julia drove the Van slowly, as Wanda and the men poured sand in front of it.

Chapter Eleven
Deep Waters

"I KNEW THERE were ice fields in southern Mars," Mark said, "but this one wasn't marked on my map. NASA knew about them since 2002, when they were discovered."

"That's one of the things we were to explore," Glen said. "NASA wanted us to pin-point them."

"That's all well and good," Jim said, "but how are we going to cross a field of ice without getting stuck in it?"

"Can we go around the ice?" Wanda asked.

"I guess we could," Jim said, "if we knew where the edges of the ice field were."

"Could we use the sand dunes?" Wanda asked.

"Right," Julia said. "We can fill these empty tortilla bags with sand from the dunes. Then we spread the sand where the Van wheels go."

"That's what we did for icy roads in Missouri," Jim said. "It will work!"

Four astronauts and a fourteen-year-old girl filled bags with sand. Hopping in the "Bucket", they rejoined the Van and Lander at the edge of the ice field. From the hill,

Mark sketched the ice field on his map with his grease pencil. Julia drove the Van slowly, as Wanda and the men scattered sand in front of it.

"Watch out!" Wanda heard Glen cry. The Van slid sideways. Wanda's heart seemed to be thumping in her throat. Wanda thought the van would never stop. The Van began to slow.

"It's over," Julia said. "We are stopped." Glen knocked on the Van door.

"Are you alright?" he asked.

"I'm not hurt," Julia said. The men poured more sand around the wheels of the Van. Jim entered the Van and took Julia's seat. He steered the Van, inching it along the sandy path on the ice field.

The Van was safely in the rocky area at the south edge of the ice field. Glen took an empty thermos and one of the alpine hooks back into the ice field.

"Have to get samples of this ice," Glen said. "It's probably water ice, but who knows what's in it." Glen climbed into the Van with his thermos of ice and the Van climbed over a large rounded ridge. Julia seemed happy to let Jim do the driving.

"This is the scalloped outer wall of a large, oval crater, named Amphitrites," Mark said. "It looks like two craters, overlapping, but was probably caused by a low-flying meteor. As the meteor struck the ground, it slid, making an oval crater," Mark said. "Barnard Crater is just beyond this one."

Again, Wanda saw sand dunes. This time, the dunes were surrounded by the large rounded hills of the crater wall. The big Van climbed and dipped over the sand dunes as they traveled the length of the oval crater.

"Using those boundary hills to guide us, I don't need my directional finder to view the path of the sun," Mark said. "But now it's time to stop for lunch."

The tortillas and hot coffee tasted great. Wanda found out she was hungry.

"We'll use the "Bucket" to travel inside Barnard Crater," Jim said. "It's about 60 miles wide, so in 30 miles, we'll be at its center. I have a rope seat to haul you up the crater wall, one at a time."

Everyone put on a helmet and climbed out of the Van to look at the 12 foot lava wall of Barnard Crater. Jim removed his alpine hooks and rope equipment from the Lander and climbed the wall. Hooks anchored his rope on the wall, every third foot.

"I'm sending down the seat," Jim said from the top of the five-foot wide wall. "Wanda, you come first." Wanda settled in the rope seat. Jim pulled her up as the chair swung in and out. She helped Jim pull up Julia. Mark was next. Glen unfastened the pipes from the top of the Van and sent them up to Jim. Then Glen tied on the

"Lander". Last, he was pulled up to the top of the crater wall. When everyone was standing at the top of the crater wall, the *"Lander"* was lowered inside the crater. Jim threw the pipes down. Each person was lowered. Last of all, Jim descended, leaving his ropes to dangle from the wall.

"We will explore the crater," Jim said, "then come back and eat dinner in the Lander."

Mark held the ultra-stratus radar machine in the *"Bucket's"* back seat, with Julia, who held Wanda. Jim drove and Glen held the tools in the front seat. Every four and a half miles, they stopped.

Jim attached the *"Bucket's"* solar panels to his radar machine, for electric power, then handed shovels to each person. The group moved rocks and smoothed sand dunes in a five foot square. Jim turned on a machine that looked a lot like a computer. A screen showed the layers of rock and ice below ground.

"We don't need to smooth out the top ground," Jim said, "but it makes the viewing clearer, and marks where we used the machine."

Looks like we're making graves, Wanda thought, as they left one smooth place to smooth another.

After reaching the crater's center, they rode back to the Lander.

"Barnard Crater is named after E. E. Barnard," Julia told Wanda. "He correctly described the salmon and gray colors of Mars in 1911, when many telescopes were not able to show the Martian true colors. He also discovered the nearest star to our solar system – six light years away. Later, it was found that the star has a planetary system like our solar system. The amazing thing is, Mr. Barnard discovered that star with his naked eye in the early nineteen hundreds."

Sitting in the sculptured chairs of the Lander, the tired group ate tortillas, for dinner. Wanda watched Glen bring Julia a tortilla and then sit down by her. *Glen is paying a lot of attention to Julia. Is he just being nice because she's new to the group?*

The walls held an oxygen tank and water container. Jim curtained off the area by the sixth chair for Julia's portable toilet from her Van. When everyone finished eating, Jim stood up.

"Let's go. According to my radar machine, the central area should have the most water. We still have three hours of sunlight."

"Jim," Glen said, "I brought the portable computer and Wanda's disks. I think we should leave the girls here. Wanda saw enough. She and Julia can study." Wanda frowned.

Chapter Twelve
Ice is Nice

"I CAN'T UNDERSTAND why we didn't reach water," Jim said, as the men returned to the Lander. He examined the pipe section with the point and looked at the holes. Jim picked pieces of ice and tiny rocks from the holes.

"The water appeared to be above the ninety-foot level, with no large rocks in the way – perfect for our pipes to reach," Jim said. "The first pipe, with small holes about six inches above its point, was threaded into the hole of the machine. The threads of the pipe and hole joined together. I stopped the machine for each section of pipe to be screwed into the end of the last pipe. When all the pipes were in the ground, I waited. After ten minutes, we reversed the machine and took out the pipes."

"I see what happened," Glen said. "We can't reach water without a larger machine. The water has to be below the 90-foot level. The radar machine showed a band of ice to be water. That band of ice could be 90-feet thick, itself."

"If we don't find water," Mark said, "we can always set up our solar oven machine to scoop ice from that covered glacier – without a slippery surface like the thin sheet we traveled, yesterday."

"Good idea, Mark" Jim said, "I saw you pack the solar oven. We'll sleep in the seats and get an early start tomorrow."

"This buried ice field," Wanda blurted out, "is just a few miles east of here and was discovered in the year 2002."

"You've been studying," Glen said to his sister.

"Julia, I'm glad we took a nap on the floor before the men came back," Wanda said. "Now we can play a game on this computer while they sleep."

"I'll get the game disks," Julia said.

"This game teaches about searching for water on Mars." Wanda giggled.

Next morning, Jim hauled everyone over the wall and out of Barnard Crater.

"I'm glad to be back in the comfortable van, with its own toilet," Wanda said as they drove east to the covered glaciers.

After half a day, they were in a smooth area at the edge of the Hellas Plains. Again they used their shovels to reach the ancient glacier. It was buried about three feet under the fine, dusty layer of dirt. Glen and Jim set up the solar oven machine as Mark looked over the map. It began collecting ice shavings.

"We'll need to come back here in a month and get the gasses and water from the machine," Jim said. "It will stop collecting ice when it reaches the full mark. By that time, we will need a larger supply. Remember, we can't recycle water when we are away from the station."

"We drive north from here," Mark said, "then head for those small craters and follow our tracks home."

"I'll report to NASA, our failure to find water in Barnard Crater," Jim said, as they stopped for lunch.

"Our machine gave a false picture of water," Glen said. "Barnard Crater has a thicker bed of gravel than we thought. It's not failure, just delay. I believe that water will eventually be found."

The next day, the caravan climbed and sank as it traveled over the sand dunes. By sunset, they reached the small craters.

"Tomorrow, we can plant the lichens," Glen said as everyone had a snack and retired for the night.

Next morning, the sun sparkled off of the bluish limestone rocks of the small craters. Mark was passing out the last of their tortillas with what Wanda thought was a satisfied look.

"Good job, Mark. You made just enough tortillas for our trip." Mark began to loose his eye. "I'll have to get a pill," Wanda whispered to her brother. "I have the signs of another migraine."

"Wanda, you should stay here in the van and rest."

"I can take a pill and still go with you. I don't want to be left behind."

"We're just going to plant the lichens in these little craters. You might as well rest."

Wanda sighed as Glen prepared to leave with the others.

When the NASA scientists found that the lichens grew so well on Mars, Wanda remembered, *they insisted that Glen plant more lichens in the Martian Southern Hemisphere. I was looking forward to planting them, myself.*

"Lichens grow in rocky places where most plants would die," Glen said. "It's a good thing we have these little craters on the edge of the Hellas Plains. These rocks should be perfect for the lichens to grow on." Glen gave everyone a bag of lichens.

"These dry, grayish, plants are really part plant and part animal," Glen explained to Julia as they left the Lander. "The outer plant part is a fungus that gives protection and holds water. Inside the lichen, the algae change the rock minerals into food for the fungus plant. Since algae have chlorophyll that gives a greenish tint, lichens were thought to be plants. We know now, they are a combination of fungus and one-celled organisms with green chlorophyll. The algae are not animals, but they aren't plants either. They have no roots, leaves or seeds like plants."

"You really know so much about lichens," Julia said.

Why is Julia acting like that? Wanda wondered. *She knows so much about lichens. She even explained to me that they grew all over the Earth – even in the arctic.* Wanda saw her brother with that silly grin on his face again. *Oh, Julia likes Glen a little more than I thought. She's even letting him tell her that people call the lichens 'Reindeer Moss', even though they're not moss.* Wanda grinned. *It's just as well that Glen doesn't have me with them. Julia can have him to herself.*

Wanda woke to find herself in her own bed at the station.

"Anyone here?" She found a note, saying the others were out planting lichens again. *I've been asleep for a whole day!*

"Why do I have to get migraines, just when we are ready to do exciting things, like planting lichens?" She asked the wall.

The wall answered!

"No," Wanda said. "It's the radio." She crept out of bed. *At least, I avoided the terrible headache by taking a pill right away.* Wanda could see the whole radio. Her vision was back to normal. She pressed the button for the loudspeaker, as Mark had done, but with shaking fingers.

"This is a warning from Station #1 - Jake Hampton speaking. An asteroid was sighted, heading for Mars. You must get to a safe place. Our lives are in danger."

Chapter Thirteen
Face on Mars

"Jake Hampton, speaking from Station #1: We sighted an asteroid, plunging toward Mars. If the asteroid continues on its way, this 700 foot rock, like a bomb, will hit Mars in three days. I have sent our crew to plant 70 rockets along the east side of the asteroid, ten feet apart. We hope to change the asteroid's course."

Wanda turned on the little computer sitting next to the radio. Her heart was beating wildly as she typed the message from Mr. Hampton. Wanda pressed a button with shaking fingers, to ask a question.

"Mr. Hampton," Wanda tried to deepen her voice. "can't you blow up the asteroid?"

"We tried. The explosion pushed the asteroid's stones apart just a little, but then they went back together. This asteroid is like the one NASA discovered in 2001. NASA found that an asteroid made of loose stones can not be exploded. A small probe named *NEAR Shoemaker* was sent to such an asteroid. After the explosion, the stones went back together," Mr. Hampton said.

"They didn't have rockets developed to reroute an asteroid, then. They were lucky the asteroid was not that close to Earth. Our asteroid will continue its deadly path to Mars, unless we can change its course with rockets. If we can not swerve this asteroid in its path to Mars with rockets, we'll send our ship to take your crew from Mars until the asteroid's crash is over. More news will be sent. Jake Hampton signing off."

Wanda pressed the signal bell with both hands, to warn the others of danger.

Twenty minutes later, the travelers rushed into the station. Wanda showed Jim the notes she made on the small computer. Jim read her notes about the asteroid, to the others.

"That asteroid can kill us," Jim said. "Even in our station, we might not survive. I'm happy you stayed at the station, Wanda." Everyone grabbed things they would need, if they had to leave the planet. Mark sat at the radio, waiting for more news.

"Wanda, gather about ten boxes of food to take. We could starve if our food is destroyed," Mark said. "Five could be cooked meat and five cooked vegetables."

"We have time to dig holes and bury the food bins," Jim said. "Then we won't have to worry about being without food. The bins open at the top. We can keep the tops of the bins at ground level. That way, the bins will be protected from space bombs - unless there is a direct hit."

"Wait!" Mark called, "Another message."

"Jake Hampton calling from Station #1: We sent our ship to the asteroid that is heading for Mars. Seventy rockets are being attached to the 700 foot asteroid. We will let you know tomorrow. Keep preparations ready in case we fail. Jake Hampton signing off."

"Jim," Wanda said, "the asteroid is only 700 feet wide. The block I live on at home, is twice that big. How could such a small asteroid do much damage?"

"It's because the asteroid is traveling at such a high speed," Jim said. "Even a straw in a tornado can pierce a tree trunk because of its great speed. Asteroids can be smaller than 700 feet and act like an atomic bomb."

"We must keep in touch with headquarters at Station #1, when we go on a trip," Mark said. "I'll take a small radio next time we travel."

"We should have a box of important things, if this happens again," Wanda said, "if a meteor comes and we don't have time to take off in a jet."

"That is a good idea," Jim said. "We'll plan a room underground for us, too, but it will take a long time to make."

"Could we make one quickly by burying the Lander?" Wanda asked. Jim laughed.

"That reminds me," Jim said, "if the rockets don't move the asteroid into another orbit, our station will likely be destroyed. We have an inflatable tent for emergencies. We need to bury that in a large bin, too. Mark, you and the girls make dinner while Glen and I put bins together and bury them. We must be prepared."

After dinner, everyone put something in the "treasure" bin. Wanda was first to lift the lid of the bin, where it lay parallel to the ground surface. She put in her backup disk of her parents' message, along with a small computer.

Next morning, Wanda dressed carefully. She helped herself to a biscuit. *I hope the news from Mr. Hampton is good,* she thought. *If all goes well, I'm going to look for water. I can make that machine push pipes in the ground, just like Jim did. Julia will help me.* Wanda decided not to say anything until she had a chance to talk with Julia, alone.

"Good news," Mark said, coming to the table with his maps. "Jake Hampton called to say the planet is out of danger. The rockets were successful." Everyone gave a great sigh of relief.

Julia came in with a jug of orange juice and everyone's cup on a tray. She put them next to the bowl of Mark's biscuits.

"Julia, want to listen to my parents' message?"

The girls watched Wanda's message at the south end of the table, munching biscuits and drinking orange juice. Mark and Glen looked over Mark's map at the north end of the table.

"There!" Glen said. "I really want to explore that area where a *Face* was once sighted."

"Glen, everyone knows there was really no face monument. Why would you want to bother with that? It's so far from here!"

Wanda and Julia listened to Mark's loud words. Glen answered in a quiet voice.

"I keep getting the feeling that this place is unusual for some reason. I just want to make sure. These formations could be eroded mountains. There might be caves. *The Face* has only been photographed from the air. Nobody's been there." He glanced over at Wanda and winked. "Besides, it's on my list of things to do."

"Jim will have to 'O.K.' this," Mark said in a softer tone.

Wanda and Julia traded glances.

"I'd like to see *the Face*, too," Wanda said. "Wouldn't you, Julia?"

"I think I would, but *The Face* is in the Northern Hemisphere. We are supposed to be exploring the Southern Hemisphere of Mars."

"What's this I hear about the Northern Hemisphere?" Jim said, walking into the green room. He picked up a biscuit and sipped his orange juice.

"I'd like to see the *Face Rock*," Glen said, between bites of biscuit.

"Well, we already did what NASA wanted us to do. We looked for water and planted lichens in the Southern Hemisphere."

"Did NASA agree to send bigger machines and tools?" Mark asked.

"NASA will send greater machinery to help find water," Jim said, "but another group will use the machines. Now NASA wants us to find the best passageway to the Northern Hemisphere. Mark, isn't the *Face Rock* just north of the Meridiani area? That's where we will explore."

"Yes," Mark said, "on the map, that path seems a good way to go north. We wouldn't have to cross the Marineris Valley or the Tharsis Bulge." *The Marineris Valley is that huge hole we saw when we landed,* Wanda remembered.

"Julia, tell me about the Tharsis Bulge. That's in the Northern Hemisphere. I only studied the southern part of Mars."

"The Tharsis Bulge is a very high place, with four mountains. Mt. Olympus is the largest in the solar system. The other three mountains are bigger versions of the mountains that formed the Hawaiian Islands on Earth. Scientists think the volcanic activity pushed out the Tharsis Bulge and caused the ground to split, forming the Marineris Valley, at the same time."

"The Meridiani area is close to Station #1," Glen said.

"That may be the way I came here," Julia said. "Station #1 has a nice group of greenhouses. I'm told you built one, Glen."

"With my family's help," Glen said, blushing.

"Julia," Mark said. "We could stock up on fresh vegetables if you think Jake Hampton would part with some."

"Of course he will. We're in this Mars mission together."

"We'll need to take our *"Lander"-trailer*," Jim said.

"And have plenty of time to bury it when we come back?" Wanda asked. Jim laughed.

For four days, Julia, Mark and Wanda made tortillas, pocket bread snacks and fruit drinks for the trip. Glen and Jim worked on organizing tools and ropes. The fifth day, they were ready to leave. Wanda glanced out the window.

"Dust Storm!" Wanda yelled.

"This one is really rattling the station," Mark said. "It sounds bad. We can't leave until it's over."

"If it's like the last dust storm, this one should be gone in half an hour," Jim said.

The dust storm was still going on, hours later, as everyone went to bed.

Two days later, the storm still rattled the station.

"Glen," Wanda said, "that dust storm has been banging on our station for three days. When will the storm end?"

"This is the middle of the summer season in the Southern Hemisphere. It's also the dust storm season. But I've never known one to last longer than an Earth year."

"A year!" Mark said. "We'll never get to take our trip. Listen! Now the dust storm is worse. The banging is louder."

"That's not the storm," Jim said. He slipped into his suit and put on his helmet. Wanda watched him pass through the first air lock door, only to return, with his hands in the air. Three strange astronauts followed with guns.

THREE STRANGE ASTRONAUTS ENTERED THE INNER DOOR OF THE STATION.

Chapter Fourteen
Problems Galore

WANDA WAS ROOTED to the floor. Three strange astronauts entered the inner door of the station. They were following Jim, with guns. Jim motioned for everyone to sit down. Wanda sat, keeping her eyes on the guns. Her hands were shaking. One of the strange astronauts took off his helmet.

"We come from the Republic of China," he said. "Our ship crash-landed. One of our crew was killed. We buried him by our wrecked ship. We want to know who shot us down."

"It certainly wasn't us," Jim said. "We didn't know when you were coming."

"We kept our coming a secret," the leader said. "We were afraid this would happen."

"Please put your guns away," Jim said. "We have no weapons. You are welcome to stay here and eat with us. We are willing to help you find out why you crash-landed."

The leader said something to his men in Chinese. They kept their weapons and searched the station. After about ten minutes, they returned and talked to their leader. He smiled.

"I am sorry to have treated you this way. I hope you understand how hard this has been for us." He motioned to his men. The men put down their weapons and removed their helmets.

Wanda saw three smiling faces topped by straight black hair.

"We accept your kind offer to help us," The leader said. "My name is Ming Tou. My men are Hon and Tang." The men bowed.

"We have extra beds," Jim said. He pointed to a bundle in a corner of the room. Taking the three men there, Jim began to untie the bundle.

"Please, let us do it," Mr. Tou said. The Chinese astronauts soon had three bunks sitting in the west corner of the room.

Mark put the beef stew on the table and set eight places. Wanda ate her food slowly, watching the strangers. As her eyes filled with a semi-circle of bright triangles, she took a pill.

"Julia," Wanda said, "I'm going to bed. I have a migraine."

Next morning, Wanda had a headache. Julia stayed with her as the men took the big rover. When they returned, they brought armloads of packages from the ruined spaceship.

"You were lucky," Jim said to the Chinese astronauts, "that you didn't all die in that crash."

"We thank you so much for helping us," Mr. Tou said. "We need to get word of this deadly dust storm to our people."

"I can radio NASA," Mark said. "They can relay your message." When Mr. Tou nodded "yes", Mark began talking to the radio. After forty minutes, he got up. "Mr. Tou, your people are in contact. Have a seat." Mr. Tou sat down and talked in Chinese. Forty minutes later, he got up.

"Thank you. My people are sending another space ship for us. The ship will be here in two years. While we are here, we will continue to explore the area. We came to set up a greenhouse on Mars and look for metals and gems."

Now, eight people sat at the long table. Mark had to move his super-conductive oven into the girls' room.

"Good chili," Jim said. "Thank you, girls."

"Julia made it," Wanda said. "I had a terrible headache."

"Very good chili," Mark said, "quite different from mine. You added more tomatoes, right?"

"Yes, and more Cumin," Julia said. "Want the recipe?" While Mark and Julia were exchanging notes, Jim and Glen were talking with the Chinese astronauts. Wanda listened.

"I am ashamed to say," Ming Tou said, "we found no bullet holes. We think the dust storm caused problems with our guiding device. We will study more, while you are on your trip to the north. Thank you so much for letting us use your radio and station."

"The Chinese guests seem happy to take care of the station while we are gone," Wanda said to Julia, "I'll feel better tomorrow. I think I just had another migraine this morning - not big enough for me to notice. The problem is, I didn't take a second pill. That pill would have prevented this horrible headache." Wanda rested until dinner.

With Julia's help, Mark served a baked chicken dinner with rice and mixed vegetables. They also made more pocket bread snacks for their trip.

"I'll be happy when we can have fresh salads with the greenhouse vegetables we're going to get," Mark said, and in a whisper to Jim, "I don't trust these Chinese." Jim smiled.

"Mark, they are fellow astronauts. They've suffered."

"Jim," Wanda said, "could we bring back some other kinds of vegetable plants besides the tomato and lettuce plants we have?"

"We could if we had a greenhouse to put them in," Jim said. Wanda saw Glen's face change. His eyes opened wide and he had that great smile.

"Jim, maybe we can build one when we come back," Glen said. "The plants will be alright in the girl's room for a short time. Our guests promised to water them." The Chinese astronauts smiled and nodded, "yes".

Wanda crept into bed, wide awake and shaking.

Next morning, as they were loading the rovers and their *"Lander"-trailer,* Wanda began to get her strings of lights.

"Glen, I'm getting another migraine! It's a big one. How can I go with you, just as we are ready to take our big trip to see the *Face Rock?*" Glen handed Wanda a glass of water with her migraine pill.

"Don't worry. You can rest in the Van. Julia, will you drive it? Jim, do you care if Mark and I ride in the "Bucket"? Then Wanda will have room to lie down in the Van."

"Julia can drive her Van, but Mark and his map should be with her. I'll drive the "Bucket" with you, and follow them. You are right, Glen, less people in the rover will give Wanda a chance to rest."

They said "goodbye" to the three Chinese astronauts and began their trip. Julia's Van led the way, pulling the *"Lander"-trailer* and followed by the *"Bucket"*. They traveled northeast, across the Hellas Plains. *I'm glad I can take off my helmet in this closed rover,* Wanda thought. *I don't want to throw-up in my helmet with this migraine.* She closed her eyes to the bright light that hurt them. Mark's voice was lulling her to sleep as he talked to Julia about their route.

"We pass through some of the windy parts of Mars where orange dust is blown away," Wanda heard Mark say. "This area shows dark lava. We see less craters. Crater walls keep wind from lifting the rusty soil." Wanda heard a rustle.

Mark must be unfolding his map, Wanda thought.

"When we get to this point," Mark said, "we head due east, then follow this path north, between the low territories of Margaritifer and Meridiani. Then drive on the western edge of Chryse Plains."

"Meridiani!" Julia's voice said. "That's where the robot, Opportunity, found proof that Mars had water in its past. I have a necklace made from those little silver-colored hematite nodules that were found there. NASA called them blueberries. Hematite only develops these crystals in water."

"That's right," Wanda heard Mark say.

"Chryse Plains is where two early robot missions to Mars took place," Julia's voice said. "I visited the Viking I and Pathfinder shrines to Tom Mutch and Carl Sagan."

"Good," Mark said. "You'll be able to find the area that holds the *Face Rock*. That area is called the 'Cydonia Tableland'. It's just southeast of the Acidalia Plains."

Wanda heard the plans for their trip. She wondered if the *Face Rock* would be like a statue she climbed when she was four.

Wanda remembered climbing the statue. Her mother ran to get her down. *Wanda dreamed that she was still climbing the statue in the park. The statue of the park general turned into the Face Rock. Wanda found herself walking on the top of the Face Rock. She climbed up its hair. Wanda jumped onto its cheek. The big Face Rock opened its eyes.* Wanda screamed.

Chapter Fifteen
Passageway to the North

"Wanda, are you alright?" Mark said, shaking her. "You must have had a bad dream."

"Oh. You're right, Mark. I dreamed I was standing on the nose of the *Face Rock* when the *Face Rock* opened its eyes." Julia laughed so hard, she had to bring the rover to a slow stop.

"I have to keep the "Lander" and "Bucket" from bumping into us," Julia said, laughing. "I'm glad to see you are really awake this time. You only staggered over for a drink of water, before."

Two astronauts entered through the double air lock doors in the back of the Van.

"Glad you stopped," Jim said, removing his helmet. He put a plastic box of pocket bread on a seat. Glen followed with the large thermos and plastic cups.

"Wanda's awake," Glen said.

"She finally woke up a few minutes ago," Julia said.

"We are just south of the Sabaea Basin."

"By nightfall," Mark added, "we reach the edge of the Meridiani Basin."

"That's where the rover called Opportunity, touched down," Wanda said. "Why don't we try to find water there?"

"That is now a memorial to the Space Shuttle Challenger Crew that died in the ship's break-up in 1986," Jim said. "We can go by and view the memorial, then try for water on the way back from our trip to see the *Face Rock*."

"After we see the memorial," Mark said, we'll travel north, between the territories of Margaritifer and Meridiani."

"Very good," Jim said. "I'm surprised we can make the trip to the *Face* in just four more days."

"Wanda, how are you feeling?" Glen asked. "You've been groggy for the past four days." Wanda looked surprised.

"Four days! I never remember my migraines lasting that long!"

"I do, but you haven't had many of that kind. We had a bad scare. The Chinese astronauts thought we shot them down. You usually follow such a scare with a terrible migraine."

"I had something to do with her long sleep," Mark said. "I put sleeping pills in her water. Maybe tranquilizing pills will help more, if taken when a migraine is expected. They could prevent it."

Mark should not have given me medicine without my knowing it, Wanda muttered to herself.

"You probably don't remember," Julia said, "but you and I slept in this Van, while the men used the trailer. All these seats fold down to make two nice beds. I'm also glad to have water for washing and a nice folding toilet. The men only have my portable toilet."

"I'll have to keep my eyes open on the way back," Wanda said, "to see everything I missed."

The travelers ate their chicken pocket bread and went to bed.

The dawn, with its blue fog, woke them. They made their detour to see the memorial and the little robot, Opportunity.

"That little robot still looks good, even after all these years," Wanda said. After taking pictures, they continued their journey as the day grew pinker. Wanda watched out the window as the sky and land changed.

"I had some great dreams," Wanda said. "Now I'm riding in a prairie full of potato-sized boulders and gravel. I see a few rocks that could pass for tables and chairs. Mark, you said this was tableland." Julia and Mark laughed.

"Glad to see you have back your sense of humor," Julia said. "With Mars being half the size of Earth, the horizon is much closer. That's why we can't see dark basins next to this plain."

"Julia, I wish I could run outside without my helmet, like I did on Earth."

"We're close to the equator," Mark said, "the temperature is only 45°. Why don't you study my map?"

"Yes, Julia said, "and see if there's anything you'd like me to drive by." Wanda looked at the map.

"Everything is so far from here." She looked out the window again. "The plains are changing. Now the ground is much rougher, with little hills and craters. Wow," Wanda said, "look at these huge craters we're coming near. Some craters have walls as big as four-story buildings. There's one, the size of a mountain – a small mountain."

"That could be a mountain," Mark said. "There are other mountains on Mars besides the four on the Tharsis Ridge."

"I don't see the mountain on your map," Wanda said.

"It's so small," Mark pointed to a tiny swirl on the map.

"The little mountain looks much better than that blot on your map, Mark," Wanda said.

"We are entering the tablelands of Cydonia," Mark said. "These formations were shaped by the wind from what was once a plains area. The wind carried away clay deposits from the plain. Oddly sculptured clay hills were left in these shapes. We have sandstone formations in the western United States. Most of these Martian formations are much larger than the ones on Earth."

"Julia, could we stop here?" Wanda asked.

"Yes, I'll just drive around this mountain."

Wanda bounced onto the floor and hit her head on the seats. She opened her eyes to find Mark putting a cold cloth on her head.

"What happened?" she asked.

"The Van went down in a hole." Wanda pushed herself up. Then, grabbing the seats on either side of her, she stood up.

"Mark, what's wrong with Julia? She's bleeding!"

Mark got his first aid kit. He took Julia's pulse and bandaged the cut on her forehead. Jim and Glen came into the Van and pushed down four seats to make a bed for Julia. Mark used the thermos of cold water to dampen a cloth for Julia's forehead. Wanda could not hold back the tears.

"She's coming to," Mark said. It was then, that Wanda noticed the snow piled half-way up the windows of the Van.

"Is that snow?" Wanda wanted to know. Glen shook his head "yes" as he looked into Julia's eyes. Wanda saw snow on the tops of Jim's boots.

Jim took the driver's seat, to slowly ease the Van up out of the hole.

"Thanks, boys," Julia said, "I'm alright – except for a headache. Good thing I wasn't wearing my helmet. It could have cracked. My head is much harder." She laughed. "That hole was a total surprise. I only saw flat plains."

"Julie, you didn't see the hole," Jim said. "because dust blew on top of the snow, making it look like the rest of the flat tableland."

"Most of this tableland is flat, except for sculptured places where the old plain was eroded away by wind or water." Mark said, "but there are a few holes. This is the first one we came to. We knew there might be snow, but I expected it to be in craters."

"NASA first discovered snow in craters," Glen said, "in 2003, from the Mars Odyssey space probe. The probe's photographs showed formations of thick snow packs and run-off places."

"Hold on," Jim said, "we're slipping backwards."

JIM SCALED THE SIDE OF THE FORMATION, LIKE A GIANT SPIDER.

Chapter Sixteen
Northern Tablelands

"We're going back down in the hole again!" Jim said. Jim tried to turn the wheels faster, but the wheels were just sinking into the sandy surface. Slowly the Van slid backward and settled down into the bottom of the hole again.

"We'll have to try pulling the Van with ropes," Jim said. "Julia should keep lying down. Glen, you and Mark and I can try pulling the Van. Wanda can sit at the steering wheel and make sure we come straight up the hill."

"Jim, it might just work," Glen said. Mark, Jim and Glen put on their helmets and tied ropes onto the front fender of the Van. Then they walked to the top of the hill.

"Alright, Wanda," Jim said, "take the brake off and slowly bring the Van forward as we pull the ropes." Wanda inched the Van up the hill as her fingers froze onto the steering wheel.

"We are keeping the Van from going backwards," Glen cried, "but it isn't moving very much." Wanda pushed a little harder on the fuel and the Van began to move forward until the back wheels were on solid ground. She stopped, but could not move her fingers from the steering wheel for several minutes. *I think I'll let the others drive from now on,* she thought.

After lunch Glen drove the Van through the tablelands.

"These hunks of rock look like old mountains," Wanda said.

"We're passing through a large circle of weathered 'mesas', or 'tables' like the ones we have on Earth," Jim said. "Some are flat on top, and some have points, where the wind shaped them."

A few more hours brought them to smaller mesas that were closer together.

"This is the group of mesas that were named 'The City'," Glen said. "Even on the ground, they look like a group of houses. I want to search this area for fossils."

Glen slowed down, then stopped by a larger mesa. Everyone put on a helmet. They walked over to an orange formation.

"This looks like the six-story red brick apartment near our house, Glen. That was a plain solid rectangle of a building."

"Yes, Wanda, it does look like the apartment."

"Let's walk around the formation's base," Jim said, "Fossils may have weathered out of its side."

"Can I follow you in the "Bucket"?" Wanda asked.

"Wanda was doing well when we practiced driving in the "Bucket"," Julia said, "and she did a great job when we slid into that hole."

"I guess you can drive," Jim said, "if Julia rides with you. It's not against the law to drive without a Missouri driver's license here on Mars. Are you feeling better, Julia?"

"I'm fine, now," Julia said, "thanks to all that care you fellows gave me."

Wanda eagerly jumped into the driver's seat of the "Bucket". After a few jerky starts, she was driving smoothly.

"You're doing well," Julia said. They followed the men.

"Here's the edge of the formation where I turn right," Wanda turned the steering wheel. "Wow, I guess I took that turn too fast." Walking along the side of the formation, the men gathered bits of rock that might contain fossils. While Wanda drove, Julia bagged the men's rocks.

After an hour, they climbed back into the Van and continued their trip to the *Face Rock* formation. The sun was low in a pink sky when the convoy reached the Face Rock.

"It doesn't look anything like a face," Wanda said, frowning.

"You have to view the formation from above, with the sun making the right shadows, for this hill to look like a face," Jim said, laughing. "The early aerial photographs were taken from that position. Later, aerial photos from different times of the day proved that this was just another ordinary formation. But we can climb this hunk of rock and clay. I'd like to see how the surface really looks."

"The *Face* would be a perfect place to plant the rest of our lichens," Glen said.

Next morning, Jim took out his ropes. He scaled the side of the formation, like a giant spider, then used his "web" rope chair to bring up the others. Glen brought five bags of lichens. When everyone was on top of the *Face Rock,* Glen showed them where to plant lichens.

"We landed in late summer, on the Southern Hemisphere of Mars," Glen said, "but in this northern area, it's late winter." Glen was almost dancing along as he put the small plants in the red soil.

"This is real tableland," Mark said. "It's almost flat in places. Where we find sunken places and rocky peaks, shadows are formed. This one shadow looks like an eye, from above." Wanda stood in the eye of the *Face*.

"I'm in its *mouth*," Julia said.

"I think the wind scooped this mouth out," Glen said. "Look! I see ice! The lichens will grow well here. Where there is ice there is moisture."

"Glen, you look like a boy in a candy store," Wanda said, laughing. Everyone helped Glen plant the last of the lichens. "Now the *Face Rock* has a moustache," Wanda said, "and eyebrows."

"We finished just in time," Jim said. "The sun is sinking."

Jim lowered everyone from the *Face Rock* in his rope chair.

"I want to climb one of those pyramid formations to the south, tomorrow," Jim said.

They were back in the *Trailer* for their dinner, when Mark turned on the radio.

"Listen to this," he said. "The group who plans to replace us at "Station #2", is on the way to Mars. Just before leaving Earth, one of the crew members was rushed to the hospital with appendicitis."

"They'll be one person short," Glen said. "NASA may want one of us to stay a few more years."

"It sure won't be me," Mark said. "I want to get home to my girl."

Last time Mark talked about this girl, Wanda thought, *He said he'd 'look her up'. Now, she's already his girl. I wonder what she would think of Mark's talk.*

"Well, we still have time to climb one of those pyramids as we return to our station," Jim said. "We can take more pictures before we go back."

After their dinner, Mark insisted that Wanda have one of his tranquilizing pills. The girls went back to the Van for the night. Wanda felt her muscles aching, but she had a peaceful feeling as she drifted off to sleep.

Next day, they headed for the pyramid, due south.

"Julia, I think that pill was what I needed to keep away a migraine," Wanda said. "But the new energy I feel is from jumping around and planting lichens, yesterday."

"I know what you mean," Julia said. "Exercise helps to keep you fit and eager for more exercise."

They passed another, large formation and a smaller crater in the Cydonia tableland. Wanda was surprised when Mark told them to stop.

"How could we be at the pyramid?" she said. "I just see a big formation, but it doesn't look like a pyramid."

"From the air," Mark said, "It looks like a pyramid, even though its corners are more rounded up close. It's the D&M Pyramid – twice the size of *The Face*."

Jim had his climbing ropes, starting up the formation. Glen followed behind, grabbing the rope, hand over hand.

"Come on," Mark said. "Grab the rope and let's follow." Julia helped Wanda hold onto the rope, then grabbed the rope behind her. For half an hour, Wanda felt like one of five spiders, crawling up a silk thread.

"Julia, I'm slipping," Wanda cried out.

Chapter Seventeen
Chinese Greenhouse

"Julia, I can't climb this pyramid any more," Wanda cried. "I'm slipping on the orange pebbles. Julia grabbed Wanda's arm.

"You're alright, Wanda," she said. "I think we've gone far enough. Jim, Wanda and I are going back down." The girls hung onto the rope as they stumbled down the pyramid formation.

"I'm sorry, Julia. I didn't want to keep you from climbing the famous Martian pyramid. The pebbles and clay that this formation is made of, are dry and crumbly. My boots keep slipping."

"I was ready to come back down. My head was beginning to hurt again. Let's look for fossils. That takes less energy."

The girls returned to the Van with handfuls of pebbles.

"Julia, I don't hear the men's voices. Can they hear us?"

"No. These short-range helmet radios work both ways. If you can't hear them, they can't hear you."

"Good. Would you help me find water?"

"Water?"

"Yes. When we get back to our station, will you go with me to find water?"

"Sounds like you have a plan, Wanda."

"I want to search little craters, instead of big ones."

"That sounds like fun. We can follow the plan secretly, when the men are busy." The girls grinned as they sorted little rocks with square, round and triangular shapes. They cleaned the rocks with sandpaper from Jim's toolbox. Then they rubbed and polished the bits of basalt, pyrite and quartz with parachute rags.

The girls showed off their collection of odd-shaped, colorful rocks as the men came to the Van for lunch.

"We scraped the rust off of these rocks," Wanda said. "Now they look blue, clear and gold, as well as orange"

"We have nice rocks," Julia said, "but no fossils."

"Some of your rocks look like chert," Jim said. "Chert has been known to contain tiny fossils. NASA can investigate them for possible one-celled organisms."

They began the trip back, on a new pathway going southeast. This time, they all rode in the Van.

"We might as well see some of the other parts of Mars on the way back," Jim said as they left the Tablelands of Cydonia.

"Then we'll head for Station #1 and stock up on fresh vegetables," Mark said.

"Look," Glen pointed. "We are on the edge of the Chryse Plains. I was hoping to see it again. This area reminded me of those deserts on Earth, but without birds and lizards."

"Yes," Wanda said. "This is the Plains where Viking I first touched down and took pictures of the rocks. I read that the machine also took dirt to analyze for life forms. Viking I is now the Tom Mutch shrine."

"In 2009," Julia said, "NASA scientists found that if Viking I could have dug down just a little farther, the robot would have found ice.

"When I was nine," Glen said, "we came through this area on our way south. Farther south, on these plains, the little robot, Sojourner, tried to analyze different rocks."

Late in the day, they traveled around three-foot tall craters in a higher Chryse Plain.

"Except for the craters, this looks like the desert I saw in Nevada," Wanda said. They came down a gently sloping area, strewn with rocks from gravel size to one foot high. Viking I stood gleaming in the late sun.

"It's hard to believe that this machine came all the way to Mars by itself in the 1970s," Wanda said. "I bet the people who saw its pictures were surprised at the surface of Mars. They used to think animals and plants lived here."

"Well," Glen said, "animals did live here. Of course, they were tiny, probably less than half an inch." The astronauts took pictures of each other, standing by the old machine.

"Jim," Mark said, "if we veer to the east a little more, we will connect with the Kasei River Valley. It will get us close to Station #1 with a smoother ride. Here it is on my map."

"Good," Jim said. "We'll drive that way tomorrow. Now we should get some sleep."

Next day, the convoy rode down the less rocky Kasei Valley where there had once been a river. Low places in the old river bank showed where streams entered the great river. It seemed as if it stretched across the entire Northern Hemisphere, from the Marineris Valley by the equator to the Acidalia Valley near the North Pole.

"Some day," Julia said, "there may be a new river filling this great river basin."

They reached Station #1, now the headquarters for Martian dwellers.

"Their station looks just like ours," Wanda said, "except for those greenhouses. They stick out in all directions from the station, like spokes on a wheel."

"Jake Hampton is the head man, and also an expert gardener," Julia said. She introduced everyone.

"Jake," Jim said, "Thanks for saving us from the asteroid last month."

"Just part of my job," Jake said, laughing. "We would have met sooner if the mission had failed. We intend building a few underground rooms for just such a future emergency. Some day, we'll have asteroids under better surveillance. Oh, there is someone I want you to meet." Jake motioned to a small astronaut. "People, I want you to meet William Runner. He was going to come to Mars with you, on the 'Freedom', but caught the flu instead."

"Hi," William said, "I just got here two days ago. Sorry I couldn't come with you."

"Well," Wanda said, "I'm sorry you were sick, but I wouldn't be here if you had come the first time. I'm glad you finally got to come." The boy removed his helmet to show hair with soft black ringlets. His skin was dark – almost as dark as Mark's. He wore a big grin. Wanda and Julia talked with William about his trip.

The travelers were invited to stay in the station for a few days before they continued their trip home. They were happy to get baths and a hot dinner. When they were ready to go, Jake had his people pack a basket with tomatoes, lettuce, carrots and strawberries. Then Jake added pea, tomato, and bean plants.

"You can grow these next to a window," Jake said.

"We do plan on building a greenhouse," Glen said. Wanda and Julia waved goodbye to William Runner.

A few more days brought them to the old rover, Opportunity. Jim directed their efforts to find water.

"We have to give up on getting water," Jim said. "Another group with larger equipment will have to tackle these water reservoirs. They are too far down for us."

A week later, they returned to Station #2 to find a greenhouse attached to it.

"Jim!" Mark said, "The Chinese have taken the station!"

Chapter Eighteen
Secret Mission

THREE SMILING CHINESE astronauts greeted the astronauts as they entered the station.

"You made a greenhouse!" Jim said.

"We had the greenhouse parts in our ship," Mr. Tou said. "I radioed Mr. Jake Hampton while you were gone. He promised to keep our secret. He offered to send us a rover for the trip to Station #1."

"Thank you for such a fine gift," Jim said. "You must take our Van. We won't need it. We will be leaving Mars soon."

"We thank you so much," Mr. Tou said. Mark and Wanda hurried to make dinner, while Julia helped Glen and Jim unload the rovers and *"Lander"*. Soon they relaxed to eat beef stew and fresh salad.

"Nothing is better than tomato and lettuce salad," Wanda said, "unless it's strawberries for dessert."

Next day, the men helped the Chinese astronauts load the Van. Wanda and Julia prepared a chicken feast. After dinner, the astronauts exchanged stories. Wanda liked

Mr. Tou's story about the boy who climbed a mountain to be closer to Mars.

"That was a true story," Mr. Tou said, blushing. "That little boy was me. I always dreamed of coming to Mars."

Early next morning, the Chinese set out for Station #1, with the extra package of disks for William Runner's computer.

"You outgrew those disks, Wanda," Julia said, "and now my rover is going back home with new owners."

"I misjudged those Chinese fellows," Mark said. "They were true to their word."

Wanda and Julia helped Glen set out the tiny plants in their new greenhouse. Wanda also made sure to charge the battery in the special machine that was to push pipes into the ground next day, for their secret plans to find water.

The men made plans for the coming astronauts.

"We're almost out of the storm season," Glen said. "but if we do have a dust storm, how will the new Martians land?"

"Since we know they are coming," Mark said, "we can contact them with the radio and guide them here." A beeping sound drew Mark to the radio.

"Here's another message. The astronaut who couldn't come with the new Martians, was the cook."

"I guess you'll want to make some of your dinners and freeze them for the newcomers," Jim said.

"Yes," Mark said, "I'll do that."

Wanda and Julia decided to have their turn at looking for water.

"Jim, we want to go sightseeing," Julia said, "while you and Glen are busy building that extra room."

"Alright," Jim said, "We won't be going anywhere. Glen and I are going to put the old Lander in the hole we dig."

"It'll make a neat place for an emergency room," Jim said. "We will only be gone a short time," Julia said. Wanda wants more driving practice."

Once outside, Julia and Wanda quietly packed the little rover with pipes and the machine. They had one of Mark's maps to find the small craters, 2 ½ hours south of the station.

Julia put her finger to her lip area. *I know she's reminding me that the men can hear us. I'm driving south. The men are working on the north side of the station. They won't see us. They don't know we took the pipes.*

"I don't hear the men," Wanda said, after a while. "That means we can talk and they won't hear us."

"Our helmet radios can let us talk, but the men are too far away to get our signals." Julia said, "They'll be surprised that we're looking in that group of small craters, for water."

"Small craters are not important to the know-it-all men," Wanda said. "They told us, small craters held less water."

"But if we find water," Julia said, "it proves that craters do hold water on Mars. You have a good idea, Wanda."

"We must really seem funny," Wanda said, "with almost a yard of pipe sticking out on each side of the "Bucket"."

The girls took turns driving over the rows of sand dunes.

"I was sure our tracks would be gone," Julia said, "after that fierce dust storm we had. But the path is still showing."

"It looks like the wind pushed these sand dunes back and forth," Wanda said, "but where we dented the sand dunes, there's still a small dent – like a faint road."

"I'm certainly relieved about that," Julia said, "I'm not sure how to use this 'sun tube' of Mark's." The girls burst out laughing.

"I'm going to have to quit laughing," Wanda said. "I'm fogging my helmet." Then the girls laughed even harder.

"When we ride to the tops of these bigger sand dunes," Wanda said. "I see the craters."

"Yes," Julia said. "the craters are about 300 yards away."

"Now the sand dunes get smaller," Wanda said.

"The ground is getting rocky," Julia said. "We are close to the small craters. The sun is still high. We should get back before dark." Julia drove between crater walls.

"Stop by that one, Julia." Wanda pointed.

Julia parked next to an older crater filled with large boulders. Beyond, were several other small craters.

"This crater is so old, part of its wall is gone," Wanda said. "We can drive right in with the machine and pipe sections." The girls walked around inside the crater.

"Such an old crater is a good place to practice searching for water," Julia said, "but I'll be surprised if we find any."

"This crater is almost the size of my back yard," Wanda said, studying the clumps of lichens growing on worn rocks.

"Your brother was smart to put the lichens on those hunks of blue rock. At night, the rocks get very cold. At dawn, the sun melts the frost on the rocks and the lichens get their daily drinks. The lichens look pretty, gray-green next to orange sand that covers everything. Wanda, look at these limestone rock slabs."

"Yes, they're a lighter color, too. Glen said they might have fossils in them." Wanda found a ten-foot clear place near the crater's back wall. "Julia, how's this place to put the pipes?"

"Good! Stay here. I'll bring the pipes in the rover."

The girls dug into the soft dirt like Jim had shown them.

"It's big enough to hold the engine," Wanda danced around the machine. "I feel like a mother turtle making a nest."

"Now we feed the pipe sections through this little engine and into the ground to bring up water," Julia said.

She and Wanda struggled to stand the pointed nine-foot pipe section on end, in the hole of the machine. They twisted the section into place. With a purring sound, the engine turned a threaded pipe section through its threaded hole, into the old crater floor.

When that section was in the ground, except for about three inches, Wanda stopped the machine. Again, the girls struggled to fit another nine-foot pipe section onto the end of the first one.

"Julia, the machine is coming up the pipe, out of its nest."

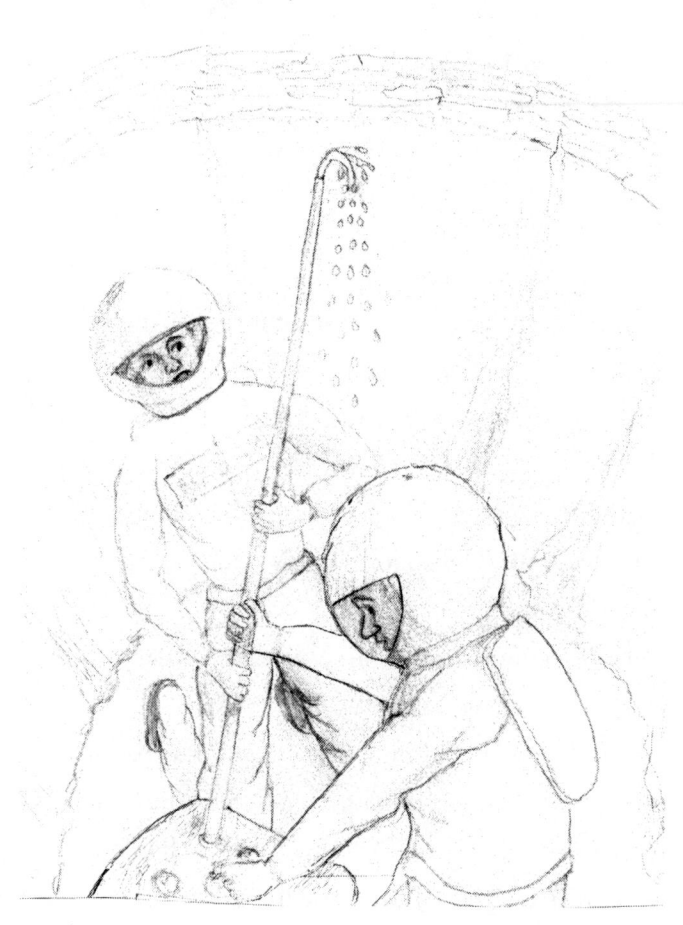

JULIA AND WANDA HELD THE PIPE AS CLEARER LIQUID SQUIRTED OUT OF IT.

Chapter Nineteen
Water for Wanda?

"Stop the machine," Julia said. "I hope we haven't ruined it. The pipe must have hit a rock." Wanda turned the machine off, then reversed it. The pipe slowly moved back up. The machine settled back down.

"Julia, our mission fails! We didn't take Jim's radar machine. It would have let us know rocks were underground. These black rocks that came up with the pipe, I'll keep for my collection," Wanda placed the rock bits in her bag.

The girls put the machinery in the little rover and drove out of the old crater.

"Maybe we should find a crater with few rocks on its surface," Julia said, "and maybe fewer rocks underground."

"There's one ahead," Wanda said, "that isn't very rocky. It is deeper." Julia parked and the girls stepped over the small crater wall and down a ten-foot incline. Again, they dug a hole, inserted the machine and began to thread the pipe sections through the machine's threaded hole. They watched, ready to turn off the machine if trouble began again. The machine shivered and screeched with the sixth pipe.

"Wanda, turn it off. We have time to try another crater." They brought up the fifth pipe section and were carrying it to the pile of pipes when Wanda dropped her end.

"Water!" They shouted to each other. A trickle of brown goo spouted from the top of the last pipe section.

Julia dropped her end of the pipe and ran back to the rover. She returned and held the pipe as clearer liquid squirted out of it. They raised the pipe just above the crater surface and unscrewed it.

"Quickly," Julia said. "Clamp the cap on the top of this pipe and use your shovel. We must cover this pipe with dirt to keep the water from freezing in it."

The girls scraped orange dirt back into the hole. *Like mother turtles, covering their eggs,* Wanda thought. Julia stuck a narrow rod on the mound of dirt. The rod was topped with a four-inch, black box.

"It looks like an overgrown lollipop," Wanda said, dancing around the mound of dirt.

"This homing device will lead us to the water pipe, with Jim's finder," Julia said as they walked back to the "Bucket".

"Let's hurry to the station," Wanda said, jumping into the driver's seat. "I can't wait to see the men's faces when they learn that we found water."

The girls followed their tracks at 60 miles an hour since they had no heavy pipes and machinery to weigh down the "Bucket". They returned to the station in a little over two hours. The men were discussing their new emergency room, eating fresh tortillas.

Julia took a bath, while Wanda swallowed a migraine pill. Wanda could hear the men talking as she lay on her bunk bed.

"That was a good touch," Glen said, "laying the Lander on its side, so one of the windows would be a skylight. Who would have thought the useless Lander could make such an emergency room for us? With any threat of asteroids, we will be safe in the underground Lander." After about ten minutes, the men became quiet.

"Didn't the girls come in?" Mark asked. "Where did they go?" Just then, Julia came out of the bathroom. Wanda got off of her bed.

"Girls, leave your suits on," Jim said. "Oh, would you put them on again? We have something to show you." Jim waited while the girls pulled their suits back on, then led them outside, to a metal slab laying on the ground. He lifted the metal slab. See? We have a ladder in this big tube, going down to our underground room." The corrugated metal sheet was rolled to make a sturdy wall for the entrance to the underground room. Wanda followed the others down the ladder.

"Come into the new room," Glen said. "The seats make good shelves, being sideways. We can store emergency food and oxygen on them." Wanda ducked into the round door and found herself standing in the side of the *"Lander"*.

"I like the window skylight," Wanda said, "but what about the window on the floor?"

"We can throw a few planks of plastic over that," Jim said, laughing.

"Wouldn't it be better to put the sled – I mean – metal window cover on it?" Wanda asked.

"I guess you're right," Jim said. Since the Lander side that curved, was now the floor, it was easier to sit on such a floor than to stand on it. As they returned to the station, the sun was setting.

"I guess this underground room will be strong enough," Wanda said. "We did come through the Martian atmosphere in it."

"Julia, you and Wanda should eat," Mark said. "I made tortillas." The girls were too tired to do anything except eat and go to bed.

"We can tell them in the morning," Wanda said.

"Yes, we can't show them your well until then, anyway."

"Our well." Wanda drifted off to sleep, thinking about the great secret that she and Julia had.

Next morning, Wanda and Julia were dressing.

"I hear the men talking and smell fresh coffee!" Wanda said."

"and Mark's cooking eggs and ham!" Julia said.

"Well, shouldn't we be ready to take the ship back, as soon as the newcomers get here?" Wanda recognized Mark's voice.

"Not so fast," Wanda heard Jim say. "We'll need to stay a while, get them settled in, and give them a tour. We should show them the memorials to Tom Mutch and Carl Sagan. The new Martians also need to see the Russian memorial near here, dedicated to Cosmonaut Terechkova, the first woman in space. We didn't even see that yet."

By the time Julia and Wanda got to the table, Glen and Jim were out finishing the underground room. Mark cooked extra dinners, placing them outside the station to freeze. Wanda and Julia grinned at each other as they ate their ham and cheese omelets.

"I think we've done about as much as we can." Jim said, entering the station with Glen. "Now we can relax."

"Good," Julia said, rinsing her breakfast dish. "We helpless little girls have something to tell you."

"We found water!" Wanda said.

Chapter Twenty
Coming and Going

"We found water!" Wanda said.

Jim stood with his mouth open.

"Do you mean to tell us that you let us babble on when you had such news? Let's go see your well."

"It's 125 miles south of the station," Julia said.

"It will take over two hours to get there," Wanda said.

The astronauts donned their helmets and piled into the little rover. Wanda sat on Julia's lap in the back seat with Glen. Jim and Mark sat in front. Wanda showed Jim their tracks as he drove.

"These tracks you left make it easier to drive," Jim said. Their trip through the sand dunes went much faster without the Lander to pull. When they came to the group of small craters, Julia gave Jim the finder device.

"This will show you the way," she said. Winding in and out among the small craters, they came to an old crumbling crater.

"There are the lichens we planted," Glen said.

"This crater is only about 50 feet wide," Jim said. "There can't be much water in it."

"That's the first one we tried," Wanda said. "We hit a rock and had to find another crater."

The finder device brought them to a newer, smoother crater.

"This crater is even smaller," Glen said.

"True," Julia said, "but finding water proves that NASA was right about craters holding water."

The men dug small shovel's full of red dirt, away from the crater's center.

"Fine job," Jim said, scraping the last of the red dirt away to find the machine with its pipe. We must report this to NASA. Mark, get this on your map." He turned to Wanda and Julia. "That was good thinking! We were trying to find a large supply of water, when all we really needed to do was find water."

Jim was able to get the machine out of the hole without moving the capped pipe. Glen uncapped the pipe just enough to get a cup of water in a thermos.

"Now the sample will not freeze," Glen said. "The water can be analyzed for mineral content." They drove back to the station singing "Row, row, row your boat". Mark held up his hand for quiet. He pointed to his small radio.

"The radio says our visitors were sighted in the upper atmosphere," Mark said. "This small radio is cracking up. I can't hear. Our visitors could be caught in a dust storm. Can we go any faster?"

Going at top speed, they reached the station in an hour. Mark settled down at the radio.

"The new astronauts made a safe landing," Mark said, rising from the radio. "They were able to avoid that small dust storm. The ship is about a mile southeast of us."

Glen called from the sink where he had been analyzing the well water.

"I must report to NASA on the tests of the girl's water," Glen said. "I found the minerals to be mostly iron, but I'm taking the sample to NASA. It may also have life."

"Life!" Wanda and Julia said together.

"Yes, I found some interesting things, possibly like our earliest microbes. Or, it could just be a chemical mixture that solidified that way. We might be able to tell from the black chert that Wanda found by the well." Glen grinned at the looks on their faces. "Fossil traces are often found on Earth, in the black chert of Australia."

"It would have to hibernate for thousands of years to still be alive," Julia said. "That would be amazing." Glen finished reporting to NASA.

"Come on," Jim said, "let's go greet the new people in the space ship. They are surely ready for us by now."

"Wait, Jim," Mark said, taking fresh loaves of bread from the oven. "You and Glen should go. The "Bucket" holds four, nicely. There won't be enough room for all of us. Wanda and I can ride back with Julia to get the baggage after you bring the new astronauts here."

"Good idea," Jim said. "Glen can wait at the ship to help load the supplies that they brought."

Jim and Glen drove off to the spaceship. Mark stirred his chili while Julia washed the breakfast dishes. Wanda unfolded three additional chairs and placed them at the table.

"Why don't we make a wagon to pull behind the "Bucket"?" Wanda asked, carrying a bundle of green plastic bin parts from the corner.

"Great idea," Julia said. While waiting for Jim to return with the new Martians, Mark and the girls put together another bin. This time, they left off the front plastic slab. The bin was placed on its back. Mark fastened extra wheels under it.

"We just made a green wagon," Wanda said, sitting in it, but it still looks like a bin, sitting on its back.

"We need to have our duffel bags packed," Mark said. "We'll be going home in that new ship. I don't want to wait till the last minute."

"Good thing the men left those extra three bunks up, after the Chinese left," Julia said. "We just need to move two of them into our room."

"Mark, two ladies and a man are coming, aren't they?" Wanda asked.

"Yes, I'll help you move those beds," Mark said.

"Bunk beds aren't as heavy on Mars," Wanda said as the three moved two beds into the girl's room. Mark was still talking about going home, when Jim and three strangers arrived.

"Amber, Marilynn and Don," Jim said, "meet Mark, Julia and Wanda. I'll show you around the station while they get your baggage."

"Nice to meet you," Julia and Wanda said together. Then they put on their helmets. Mark drove the little "Bucket" over small sand dunes, following the path that Jim made earlier.

"Those ladies are pretty," Wanda said, "Would you say they are your age, Julia?"

"Yes," Julia said, "Amber is about 21, but Marilynn seems younger. There's the spacecraft. Isn't it beautiful?" A 60 foot silver ship gleamed with the pink of Martian sky.

"It's much bigger than the one we came on," Wanda said. "and I'm going to enjoy our return trip to Earth. *But I'm going to miss Julia, when we get to Earth,* Wanda thought. *I wish I had a sister like her. Mark is so quiet, after being such a Jabber-box all morning. I wonder what he's thinking.* Wanda tapped Julia on the shoulder and pointed to Mark.

"What's wrong, Mark?" Julia asked. "You haven't said a word since we left."

THEY SAID THEIR GOOD-BYES TO MARK. WANDA HAD TEARY EYES. "I FEEL LIKE MARK IS OUR BROTHER," SHE SAID.

Chapter Twenty-One
Goodbye Mars

"What's wrong, Mark?" Julia asked him again. "You haven't said a word since we left."

"There's Glen," Mark said. Wanda saw Glen standing by the ship, waiting for them with the baggage.

I know Mark is avoiding the question, Wanda thought.

"Isn't this a nice ship?" Glen asked. "We have to come back for more baggage, later. We'll take a tour then." Glen's eyes opened wider. "Wow, that was a smart idea! You made a wagon!" Glen put the baggage in the wagon and jumped in the back seat of the *"Bucket"* with Julia. Wanda smiled from the front seat.

I wonder if Julia knows I sat up here so she and Glen could be together. They drove to the station as Glen listed the great things in the new ship. Suddenly, Glen stopped talking. For five minutes, they rode in silence.

"Mark," Glen asked, "what's wrong? You're too quiet." Mark shook his head like a dog shaking water from its fur.

"I just had a shock," Mark mumbled. "Did you get a good look at those women?"

"No," Glen said. "They had their helmets on."

"Well," Mark said, "the one named Marilynn ... I know her. She's the one I was going to telephone when I got back home."

"That's a tough deal," Glen said. "She's just coming and you're going."

"That's the trouble," Mark said. "I'm not going -- I mean, I can't."

"They need a cook," Julia said, "But I thought you were in a hurry to get home."

"Are you sure you want to stay?" Glen asked. "You don't have to."

"Yes," Mark said, "I -- I do – but let me tell them. These new people might not like me."

"NASA will like it," Julia said. "They let me stay longer when they expected William Runner to come. They needed a teacher. I'm sure glad Wanda decided to come to Mars." She smiled at Wanda and patted her on the back.

They reached the station and popped through the doors. Wanda removed her helmet.

"Mark's chili smells so good after my musty suit," Wanda said. "I'm hungry."

"Dinner's ready," Jim said, "and on the table."

The new astronauts needed no special invitation. They dived into the crusty bread that Mark and Wanda had baked that morning.

"Mark James?" the new Martian, Marilynn, said, "You are the Mark I dated from the university." She smiled.

"That's right," Mark said, smiling back.

Mark looks like he's feeling better, Wanda thought.

"This chili is delicious," Don said. "I wish Al could have come. He was going to do the cooking for us."

"I can cook," Amber said, "but not without a cookbook. Would you write this recipe for me, Mark?"

"What would you say," Mark asked, "if I told you I wanted to stay and cook for you?"

"That would be very kind of you," Don said, "I'd really like another man around here -- no offense, girls."

"You really want to stay on?" Jim asked.

"Yes," Mark said. "they'll need help with cooking, maps, and setting up their equipment."

"Once we're set up," Don said, "we'll have everything running smoothly. Marilynn is the fossil expert and Amber is our medic and chemist. I'm the pilot and gardener. We plan to put together several greenhouses while we look for fossils. Mark, Jim says you are a mapmaker and radio man, too. We really do need you."

"We will also be searching for water – in the large craters, with bigger machinery," Amber said. "Congratulations on finding water and possibly, life. Glen told us you girls did it. Jim, your findings about the ice and gravel will ensure our success. NASA is sending the larger probing tools for us."

"We'll show you around the planet, before we take your ship back to Earth," Jim said. "Tomorrow I'll drive you to our well – the one the girls made."

"Oh," Wanda said, I have black rocks from the crater near where we found water. Marilyn, they may have fossils in them. Would you like to see them?"

"We really need Mark to cook for us," Marilynn said, looking at Mark.

I guess, Wanda thought, smiling, *Marilynn, the fossil expert, has her head in the clouds, just like Mark.*

For the next week, the astronauts unloaded equipment from the large spaceship. Another little rover was put together.

"I guess we're ready to explore the three Martian shrines to the Americans, Carl Sagan, Tom Mutch, and the Russian Cosmonaut Terechkova," Don said.

After belongings were in place, two little rovers went sight-seeing to the Russian and American shrines. Two weeks later, Jim decided it was time to leave. They said their good-byes to Mark. Wanda had teary eyes.

"I feel like Mark is our brother," Wanda said to Glen.

Jim took control of the spaceship and began the slow climb to reach near orbit. They stayed in orbit, gaining speed until they were able to break out. Wanda watched Mars grow smaller as they sailed back into space.

Wanda floated over to relax in their exercise room. She strapped herself onto one of three bicycles and listened to the others talking as she peddled.

"I have a new daughter I haven't seen yet," Jim said, "except from pictures over the computer."

"I don't really have a family to come back to," Julia said. "That's why I easily stayed for an extra term – almost two years."

"You must come home with us," Glen said.

"Yes," Wanda said. "You already met our parents on the computer messages." Wanda noticed Julia's face redden. *Julia is blushing. Glen has a silly look on his face like Mark had.* Wanda grinned. *Mark and Marilynn aren't the only ones who make a cute couple. Julia will be a great sister-in-law.* Wanda and Jim left the exercise room to Glen and Julia who were riding bikes together.

"Jim, I feel like I'm ready to learn to be an astronaut. Do you think I'm old enough for those special Saturday NASA classes? I'm almost sixteen years old," She said, smiling.

"You certainly are more grown-up than when we started for Mars, three years ago," Jim said, smiling. "I was surprised when you insisted that our whole group be rewarded for finding water. You are the one who really didn't give up."

"Jim, I couldn't have done it without everyone else's work. I enjoyed being a working member of the group, even though my brother likes to baby me."

Wanda smiled, then swam to the small room she shared with Julia. *I wonder how my friends, Latonya and Sue are doing since I wrote that list with them – "Things to do on Mars". I'll have to bring them the news that we covered most of the items on our list. It will be good to see them again, especially Sue's big brother.*

Wanda was checking the parachute silk inside her duffel bag when Julia entered the room.

"Julia, I'll have plenty of time to sew that red and white bath robe, now. But I won't be able to wear such a robe in space. I'd be flapping like a bird." Julia smiled and nodded with a faraway look on her face. "When we get home, I'll look beautiful in a red and white robe, Julia – and you can teach me some of those sewing tricks you know."

Wanda was interrupted by little triangles in a semi-circular string. She left Julia daydreaming in her bed bag.

Even after taking Mark's pills to prevent migraines, Wanda thought, *I still get one.* Without saying a word to anyone, she floated to the pantry of the spaceship. Taking the pill bottle from her necklace, she captured a pill. Drinking from a small bag of water, Wanda swallowed the migraine pill. She then drew a bag of coffee from the super-conductive oven. *Too much coffee will make my heart race, Mark told me, but a few cups (bags) of coffee will help get rid of the migraine faster.* She smiled to herself as she relaxed, floating alone in the exercise room. Several minutes later, Wanda heard the others coming. She strapped herself into a bike.

I can have a migraine without the migraine making me an invalid – and nobody needs to know.

The End